Lichtenstein

Lichtenstein

Seth Anawalt

TATE PUBLISHING & *Enterprises*

Lichtenstein
Copyright © 2009 by Seth Anawalt. All rights reserved.

No part of this publication may be reproduced, stored in a retrieval system or transmitted in any way by any means, electronic, mechanical, photocopy, recording or otherwise without the prior permission of the author except as provided by USA copyright law.

The characters and incidents portrayed, and the names used, in this book are fictitious. Any similarity to any character, incident, name, or biography or any person (living or deceased) is purely coincidental and unintentional.

The opinions expressed by the author are not necessarily those of Tate Publishing, LLC.

Published by Tate Publishing & Enterprises, LLC
127 E. Trade Center Terrace | Mustang, Oklahoma 73064 USA
1.888.361.9473 | www.tatepublishing.com

Tate Publishing is committed to excellence in the publishing industry. The company reflects the philosophy established by the founders, based on Psalm 68:11,
"The Lord gave the word and great was the company of those who published it."

Book design copyright © 2009 by Tate Publishing, LLC. All rights reserved.
Cover design by Cole Roberts
Interior design by Joey Garrett

Published in the United States of America

ISBN: 978-1-60799-423-7
1. Fiction / Horror
2. Fiction / Suspense
09.07.27

Table of Contents

Preface 7

Prologue 9

A Strange Welcome 19

The Novice 31

Night of Blood 45

Trapped 55

Dark Bride 71

Survival 83

Dance of Death 93

The Curse 103

Vienna 115

Riding the Storm 133

Avenging Root 147

Epilogue 167

Final Note 169

Preface

Midnight

Sunday, March 16, 2008. I begin this account with some apprehension. Will the story be believed? If so, might others seek the meaning of the words, people, setting, and plot as I have done? Here I must confess to my craft, or better care. For should I say I lived the tale, as through a portal set in nature, found by chance, who would but wonder? Better to say I had a dream and thus was carried back in time to another realm. I tried to forget; God knows I tried. They haunt me still, those words, voices. I remember well, too much it seems. I must be free of the thing or go mad! There you see, my state! Let the world decide. I am resolved. My part is merely to write it out: all I recall of that dreadful vision. The names are changed, the places too. What then? The record wants to live, and I to let go of the awful weight! Yet one should caution those who pry, as I once did: tread lightly here. The way is fraught…

S.A.

Prologue

Night Entry

Margaret and Rosemary served from the kitchen of the great stone castle high on the hill. The men, back in the camp below, had been hard at work that day in the woods and for a month since, readying the house and grounds for the coming winter. A gypsy band, they were accustomed to coming in August each year on the word of the owner, Victor von Lichtenstein, who paid them well and was used to having a feast in celebration of the finished work. They would leave in the morning, the sisters knew, and expected only to help that evening before being sent to their camp on the moor.

"Drink, Victor, to the honor of your kingdom!" Bruno Kraus jested in a jovial manner.

"To my honor then, and not yours," he replied, slapping his guest on the back as he emptied the mug of ale. He enjoyed treating his company so, often in sport, but always with the knowledge that he alone was master.

"Mine is my own, and I keep it well!" Bruno rejoined in the same merry tone. They sat to the head of a long wooden table lined with men of like bad character. No gypsy vagrants were present, excepting the sisters who served with the women and so were of notice.

"And well, as you say, I'd get me one of these maids to bed."

"A merry chase!"

"But nay, a catch!"

"You'd have my aid?"

"Bruno, my friend, the very thing!"

They spoke without being heard above the clamor of bawdy talk, the clashing of drinks, and loud guffaws. The fire crackled and blazed, reflecting the red cheeks of the men. All were happily drunk, and none cognizant of Bruno's scheme.

"You shall have your maid! I'll need only the keys."

"What! And how's this?"

"An old trick. Just watch for the girl to leave on her way upstairs. A room, I think, is in need of service."

"The end room on the left, say," Victor followed, handing the keys to the eager accomplice. "And," he added, catching his arm, "the pretty one!"

"Who else for such a great man as yourself?" he flattered and left for the kitchen.

Thus they were caught as doves in a snare. Yet, one alone would carry the keys, the younger being struck with a sudden fever. The one was Margaret. She, the flower of youth laid bare, was forced to yield, to suffer the pain of a rude assault. Then, vowing to kill her father should she tell, he left her alone and rejoined the crowd.

Ere long, the girls were sent down the mountain, the one to suffer a week of illness, the other a month of unbearable silence. Her mother was first to discern the truth—the usual period passed without blood. Her father, unable to wrest a word from a daughter who feared for his sake, was beside himself with anger and shame. They'd left the castle a month earlier and were camped by a river east of the nearest town. Autumn was nigh. Night came on, revealing the countless stars of heaven, the pain of the day given over to sleep. Soon they would venture south, all but one, that is: she who departed at midnight and in her misery made her way in search of asylum.

The child, born May 15, 1785, christened

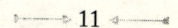

Earl Hildebrand, was put up for adoption in the summer of that year and came, by fate, to the hands and rule of the very man who'd abetted his birth.

"Now I've got you!" Bruno Kraus declared to the puny babe laid out by his side. "Earl Hildebrand, eh? Huh! You shall be Earl Kraus, do you hear?" Feeling the jolt of the voice and wagon, the child cried louder. "Cry! That's right! You'll learn to mind me. And won't he pay dear for you, young rascal!"

So, as avowed, he kept his honor, taking advantage of Victor's sin, yet doing so wisely, feigning friendship whilst coveting the keys he'd borrowed that night. The child would grow. He could use a servant. Each month the money came from Victor. In due course the boy would become a man, of age to inherit! And all that stood in his way?

Summer came. Earl Kraus, to be known as Earl Lichtenstein, had turned eighteen. Bruno must wait for three more years. Yet he grew impatient. The murder would be easy. What better way than a knife in the back? Swift, silent, unexpected. The day arrived.

"Get on with you! There's work to be done. You're trouble enough to clothe and feed. How many years have I kept you? Eh? Speak up!"

"Eighteen," Earl acknowledged.

"Eighteen!" He glared. "And you'd best be worth my while today."

The words pursued the servile son as he left the table and foul company. He'd long since learned to hold his tongue; such was his lot. What use to speak?

"Dumb as an ox!" Bruno swore to himself. "And still too young. Well, I'll wait no longer. Confound him! I want that will, and I'll get it!" he flared, shaking the table.

Earl, unaware, was whistling a tune on his way to the stables.

"Saddle my horse! Be quick about it!" the familiar voice came from behind.

Inside the barn, Earl patted the mare's side and stroked her nose as he tightened the saddle and set the bit. He understood horses and beasts of burden; they, like himself, ate to work and worked to serve—all he'd ever known of life.

"That'll do," Bruno said, returning and taking the reins. "You're on your own. And don't let me catch you slack, or I'll tan your hide! You get me?"

Earl nodded. What matter? His life was the same. He was part of nature—the world he looked after. Every rock, tree, and tool was his friend; the creatures that peopled the farm, his family. Supple and strong, he might have bettered his own in a brawl. Many a time he'd felt the lash or sting of the crop. But why react? Were not the oxen urged by his hand? Did they complain? All the same, he was glad to watch him go, to have the place to himself for a while, if only a day.

The rider galloped across the moor. He wasn't alone. Others had come to the annual bash. They filled the great hall with their usual revels, a fight breaking out here and there, much to the host's satisfaction. He, Victor von Lichtenstein, head of castle and company, exulted in shows of weaker men.

"Friends! A toast to absent wives!"

"To absent wives!" they bellowed, downing their brews in jovial pride. Another fight erupted, the two men rolling on the floor in front of the fire.

"What say you? Shall I cast the rogues in and teach them some manners?"

"Teach them!" a roar went up.

"I shall, by Jupiter!" In a single bound he held the men by the necks and bid them kiss the waiting flames. "What? Are you cowards or dogs to roll about my hearth? Kiss it, I say!"

They winced, pressed near the searing heat,

each on his knees, unable to resist the powerful grasp.

"No!" one cried. His eyebrows singed.

"Have mercy!" the other pleaded in pain.

"Cowards!" he spurned, releasing his hold. "And dogs! Who invited you hence? Be gone, I say, ere I change my mind and cast you in whole!"

Rising with caution, they edged away and across the hall, spurred on by the jeers and taunts of the pleasured crowd.

"Hurrah!" they cheered as the door slammed shut, the two cast out by a ready bunch.

"Let it be a lesson to those who come unbidden!" he warned. Then he smiled and laughed with a hearty roar.

"To your house and health!" One saluted.

"Here, here!" they shouted, standing in unison with mugs raised high. The party wore on with more raucous acts and drinking bouts till, one by one, they slumped in a drunken stupor throughout the hall, all but Victor and the guest to his left. Did he trust the man? He'd come with intent; that was plain.

"Out with it, man! What now? The boy, he's giving you pains? Good for him!"

"Could we have a word?"

"More money is it? Your fortune increased?"

"What fortune? Nay! But yours protected!"

"Well, if I must." He rose and looked about the hall. "The drunken swine!"

"Sport for a night?"

"A brief distraction."

They left and went through a hall to the study. "Damned business! I should never have touched the girl!"

"Ah, but you did and had your way, as ever."

"True. And the boy?"

"He'll soon be a man."

"A man? What sort of man without my guidance?"

"Your son all the same."

"My son is Karloff, the only one who can take my place."

"And where then is he? Off getting supplies or a gypsy wife?"

"The former, though I wish the latter."

"It seems he has little taste for women and ale."

"He'll find a wife, or I'll get him one! What of it? You have the bastard son, your money each month. What more do you ask?"

"But this, a testament in your hand, that Earl be given his right should Karloff die."

"You presume on my patience!"

"I merely advise."

"And what do you gain?"

"The will is yours to write as you like. I think only of Earl; his would be the increase, not mine. Besides, Karloff is like to live and have sons. It is but a precaution to guard your estate."

Hmmm, he thought, *better it never become my brother's. And Heinrich, my faithless son, will get nothing from me.*

"Well?"

"All right! I grant your point."

"There you are then; a quill for the ink!"

"You'll witness?"

Yes—he nodded in silence—*more than you know.*

Though not drunk, the ale had had its effect. He missed the subtle hints of danger: the peculiar timing, the hidden motive, the ready hand and dagger. "That should do," he observed. "There, see for yourself."

He took the sheet and appeared to strain.

"What's the matter, man?"

"Look," he said, coming round the desk and laying the sheet on the table.

"At what?"

"This part here." He pointed with his left forefinger while drawing and striking with his free right hand.

"Why, you...you!" he stammered, straining as to take him by the throat. But the knife had hit its mark. The struggle was brief. Soon man and blade were dropped to the floor.

"I'll take this," Bruno said, folding the will and placing it safely in his pocket. "You may keep the dagger."

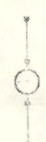
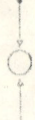

A Strange Welcome

Afternoon Entry

A tall, athletic man with piercing gray eyes set beneath jet-black brows, an aquiline nose, thin, pale lips pressed firm, a black velvet cape, and crimson vest with silver buttons whipped his team of horses in a frenzy of energy that carried the lone rider and wagon over the mountain road bending upward to the castle that sat atop a ridge looking north into a winding canyon and south toward the neighboring town from whence the traveler came. To the east stretched a broad band of forest that wrapped around the canyon at either side. Westerly, beyond the trees, a vast plateau bounded in by rugged mountain ranges on the far horizon flanked the canyon's other side, the deep gorge running a mile west of the castle before curving due north.

Within the house a fire blazed in a parlor where sat a young couple on a glossy leather couch of burgundy tone and royal mahogany.

The woman's hair curled about her forehead and neck in long blonde tresses, her bright blue eyes shining in the light of candle and fireplace, her fine milky complexion evident in bared neck and forearms. She was in love and, like other women newly engaged, radiated her joy in smiles and laughter and a sort of innocent trust.

Her companion, an impressive man with sleek dark hair that came to a point at the fore and resembled the crown of a falcon, well-set eyes and mouth, handsomely rugged face and jaw, powerful shoulders and arms, and a stature exceeding most men of his age, raised his glass of wine.

"Here's to many years of happiness, my dear!"

She imitated his action, pressing the smooth glass to her lips. "But, Henry, do you think your family will like me, accept me as I am as you do? It's difficult to grasp."

"What? Your engagement to a Lichtenstein? We are human, after all. Though I've told you, ours is a peculiar line, unusual as my brother's absence. I was certain he'd have been here by now…" The words trailed off into an absent reflection as the speaker reclined his perfectly-shaped upper body against the couch and gazed out the window.

Muriel noticed early on in their relationship this tendency of his to lapse into sudden reveries. Here, seated in the home of his birth, she saw the connection, how it was always when the subject of his family came up he'd be apt to drift, to recede into some other place. She'd thought it a weakness at first and more so with time. When he'd finally proposed three months ago, she'd suggested the trip to his ancestral home, hoping somehow it would ease his mind.

"Henry, I've lost you."

"I'm sorry. It's this house I suppose, just as I remember. Not a thing altered, not even Franz, the old butler. But where is Karloff?"

As in answer, the crack of a whip and clatter of wheels made Muriel sit upright.

Odd, she thought, *to be startled like this.* The sound grew in intensity. A warm thrill ran though her body. She pressed close to Henry, grasping his hand.

"The spell of this place is yet present, I see," he said as they stood and walked to the entry hall. "It was so when I was a child and when I finally left ten years ago; it will ever be so, I fear."

"Fear what?"

"What I've failed to confess, to acknowledge—"

Before he could finish, the doors swung open, revealing a man who resembled the speaker in build and countenance. "Ah, my long lost brother, home at last! I've been expecting you. Franz was waiting at the station, I presume."

"We made it all right," Henry replied. "But how did you know?"

It seemed to Muriel the doors had opened by magic. Were her eyes deceived? Then the face—the pale reflection of Henry.

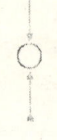
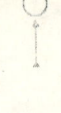

"No matter, Heinrich. Tell me, what is it you wished to confess to the lady?" A piercing glance gave way to a subdued smile, the elder brother placing his gloves and whip aside in a whirl of motion that added to Muriel's sense of intrigue.

Henry, however, was unmoved by the display. The two shook hands, a prompt, cool, reluctant performance. "Karloff, allow me to introduce my fiancée, Muriel. I trust our stay will be a pleasant one."

He gave no reply but reached out and took her hand, seizing her attention, her eyes, her soul. In an instant she was bared before him, strapped with cords to a slab of rock, unable to resist. The vision faded, and the words, "A pleasure!" made her blush as the hand was retracted. "What a beauty you've brought, a gift from Vienna! I'd know more of you. But first,"—he glanced at a side door—"enter, Franz!" The door creaked, and in came the butler.

"You called, sir."

"Prepare the table. Bring the best wine and crème brûlée for dessert."

"Very good, sir."

"You must be hungry after your journey. Let us dine. And you shall give me news of Austria."

"The world that ever advances, while here all remains as it was."

Henry's response, coupled with knowing looks, added to Muriel's curiosity, especially in view of the strange welcome.

"And so it shall! Or have you forgotten yourself, my brother? But dinner awaits. I'll join you shortly." Turning, he moved with effortless steps away and up the marble staircase opposite the main doors. A wolf cried from afar, and then another, and soon a chorus of howls followed. Muriel took Henry's arm.

"There's cause for alarm," he admitted. "I should have told you the reason I left this God-forsaken place."

"Reason?" she asked.

"Listen to me. Behave as though nothing is wrong, regardless of what may occur. And whatever you do, avoid looking long at Karloff's eyes. Trust me! Be strong, as I know you are, my love. All will be well."

"What can you mean? I thought..."

"That I came from a noble family? Noble it was. My forbearers settled this land in the thirteenth century, made it green and fruitful. But every family has its secrets—hidden mysteries of the past, bad strains that run like rats through grain or wolves at stray lambs; such it is with us."

"I don't understand."

"That is my fault for hiding my family history in shame. Too late, however; we're here and must make the best of things. Tomorrow we'll find a diversion—get away for a while. What do you say?"

"I suppose, if you like," she consented, pressing her cheek to his shoulder.

In the dining room the light was dim, four lone candles, one at each wall, providing illumination. As they sat down at the table, Franz came from the kitchen bearing a bottle of wine.

"Franz, there you are, good fellow!"

"Your wine, sir," he offered, pouring three glasses and leaving without a word.

"I'll be damned if he isn't a different man!"

"And I, Heinrich? Am I also changed as you imply?" The voice preceded the form of her fiancé's sibling, who moved in the same easy manner into and about the room, pausing before the cold fireplace, his face bent on the readied grate. Lifting his velvet cloak, he whirled round, sweeping downward as he turned and stopping back to the opening with arms extended, showing the inner red of the great cape, his eyes dancing with wild excitement. He stepped aside, revealing a roaring fire where before was nothing but darkness.

"No, Karloff, you are not changed." He frowned. "Ever the magician, practicing sorcery our forefathers should have abandoned generations ago. Why do you persist?"

"Why do you doubt? What power would you say put the sun in the sky? Nature, of course! Haven't we then in our mastery of the secret arts—the hidden forces of nature itself—come to fulfill our destiny?"

"So you would have me believe. But what of the real danger of this path? How many in our family have suffered the curse of black magic—spirits that came to possess their own souls?

How many have died in the fires you seek to preserve? Or am I mistaken?"

"You are not mistaken. You are simply naïve," the accused sibling replied, his body erect and head held high, his proud gaze fixed on the questioner, the deluded brother who'd come at last to be in his control. "Nonetheless, you as well are a Lichtenstein, one of a select family and unique bloodline. Thus, you are destined to understand; this is your duty, as mine."

"Duty? Surely you jest!"

"On the contrary. I commend your effort to claim your rightful place." Muriel watched as their host looked aside. Again, the entry of Franz, the moment his name was called. He carried a silver tray, which he set on the long cherry-wood table. "Behold," Karloff declared, "the pride of nature! What power made it possible, do you think? A perfect specimen of wild buck shot with a single arrow while high in the air and roasted in the same fire you would call magic. Very well! As you see, it is for our good."

Wishing to avoid a dispute, Henry consented. "Then let us eat and speak of other things."

Karloff raised a glass southward in salute to the sun and pronounced in response: "Those who've carried the sacred flame, preserving the way of wisdom, I honor you! And now, Heinrich, as you say, let us speak of other things."

Again, Muriel held a glass, touching the sweet liquid to her mouth. Then began a pleasant conversation, familiar and without strain. No mention was made of magic or talk of the wonders she'd witnessed. It was as though the fire had been set and lit by Franz, who'd only just now added a piece of wood. Had he opened the front doors as well? Dinner and dessert came and went. She was happy and satisfied. Soon she felt drowsy, lulled by the sound of the deep voices.

"Heinrich, I see my fair guest is ready to retire to her chamber, though tonight it will be difficult to rest. The moon is waxing. I warn you both, stay within these walls; by no means venture outside. I cannot promise protection if you do." He held her gaze. She was in his command. The words were meant for her. She'd ceased to fight. All she could think of was sleep.

"Sleep...sleep..." Was it Henry's strong arms that carried her up to bed? Had she walked on her own? Swiftly, she passed to a land of dreams, beyond the familiar peace and safety of her beloved Vienna. A heavy mist enveloped her body, the cold earth wet beneath her feet.

Before her lay a foreign landscape, stone pillars rising out from the fog as she wandered ahead, the sounds of wolves on either side. Yet, amidst the fog, she could neither see or be seen by the frustrated pack. Her foot stumbled on a bare slab. There within reach stood a tombstone of marble. The mist began to clear as she read the inscription:

> Karl von Lichtenstein
> Grand Master
> 1406–Unknown
> All Who Approach Beware

As her eyes lowered, the gravestone moved, and out rose a ghastly white form with features resembling those of Henry and Karloff. The face morphed into a half-human, half-skeletal fiend with blood-red eyes. It rushed upon her in silent fury, throwing her into a flight of terror. Back through the fog she ran, wild, frantic, hands outstretched in desperation. Someone caught her, pulled her near, wrapping his cape around her frame. The sounds faded. A wind blew over. The cloak flew open, and she awoke!

An enormous moon hung in the sky, its yellow light bathing the room in which she lay. Needing air, she got up and went to the window, flinging it open and taking long drafts in a kind of abandon. Revived, she found her vision drawn downward to a stark figure that stood attracting her gaze. It was Karloff, his bright eyes gleaming in the night. He seized her soul and held her entranced. She could neither move nor break the spell. A mist came over him. The vision faded. Collapsing in bed, she gave way to a fitful sleep.

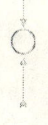

The Novice

Twilight Entry

The Convent of Saint Ann enjoyed a panoramic view: northwest to the old county seat of Steinburg; west to the mountains running north into the foothills and moorland region that covered a vast area, including the town; northeast to a canyon and farther mountain range beyond that reached northward to a dense forest flowing down from the mountain's lower regions and spanning an area to the opposite west side of the gorge that enveloped the old castle built centuries earlier by Otto von Lichtenstein, descendent of traveling gypsy magicians and great-grandfather to Karl von Lichtenstein.

Toward this castle, situated due north of Steinburg and visible only on clear days from Saint Ann's, a novitiate prayed, pleading to God for the soul of her son, Karloff. Then there was Heinrich, the younger son she'd sent away—saved from the family curse. The familiar footsteps of her friend and superior brought her round and out of the meditation.

"Christina! What is this burden you carry? Tell me. Is there no way I can aid you?"

"Oh, Theresa, I wish I could say. I've this conviction, here in my heart. Heinrich, my son; something has happened. I know it!"

Somehow the words recalled her own trial: her father's death when she was a girl, her consequent decision to become a nun. She was younger, in fact, than Christina, though her elder in rank. "You mustn't fear. God is watching over Heinrich."

"I warned him against returning; I was right to do so. But my eldest son, Karloff, no matter my prayers or pleading, Victor had his way with the boy."

"Yet, Victor is dead."

"Too late! When I saw the extent of his influence, Karloff was beyond my reach. Nevertheless, I knew. I realized I could save my son Heinrich."

"But he is safe there in Austria. And you are safe with us at Saint Ann's."

"He has come! I feel it, here in my heart. Had he written, Karloff would never have told me."

"I see. So you wish to go and find out."

"I must! I must know he is well! And it could be, perhaps, that Karloff is changed. How I've prayed for him!"

Theresa looked with compassion at her sister in Christ. She'd been impressed with the unusual zeal of the novitiate during the initial months of her trial period at the convent. Their consequent friendship only served to deepen this regard. No task was too hard, nor penance severe, or any spiritual discipline; all was joyful sacrifice. She hadn't in her many years at the abbey witnessed such zeal of faith and devotion.

"We will venture, you and I, tomorrow!" she resolved. "Ours is a sheltered life. Long have we prayed for this house from which you came. I saw your coming as a sign. And I won't have you filled with doubt or the valley with fear."

"Thank you, Theresa!"

"We'll have to ask Mother Germane, of course. For the present, let's put our thoughts from the castle and fix our eyes on brighter things. We'll commit to God our holy mission and trust in his mercy."

As she spoke, other eyes—keen and penetrating as a hawk's—focused on two specks atop the convent wall far to the south. Lifting his great cape like the wings of a giant bat, he began to beat the air with intense energy. A sudden pulsation, on an otherwise calm morning, caused the two nuns to pause. High above the northern castle, they perceived a reddish glow; it flared out as a flame and vanished.

That instant, Muriel woke from a dream in which a phantom bird had found her alone on a high tower and, swooping down, sought to carry her off. She heard a knock.

"Henry!" She sat up, the spell of her dream broken. In a rush of relief, she was at the door.

"What's this?" he asked, overwhelmed by her desperate embrace. She eased from his shoulders and smiled. He was with her, the nightmare past. He read her countenance. "Ah, it's this place, isn't it? This house, this cursed ground! I tried to tell you. But my brother, I fear he's worse than ever."

"I saw him last night in the back. He was there in the mist; I could swear!" Leading him to the window, she pointed. An empty yard flanked by gardens and a path running north from the house toward a cliff met their view. "But the wolves, the graveyard!"

Henry wrapped his arms around her and pressed his head to hers. Bringing her gently about, a hand to either shoulder, he beheld her with earnest. "No, it wasn't a dream but my father's effect. I saw him too, from my window at night, when I was young, watched him standing there in the moonlight. They're alike, those two. But enough gloomy talk! You must be hungry, for you barely touched your dinner. Come; get dressed. I'll wait for you in the dining room."

She was, in truth, famished. And the breakfast, served by the same inscrutable butler, helped to calm her nerves. No fire blazed in the hearth, she noticed. And no trace of the former fire was evident. Nor did their mysterious host appear; he was absent, like the flame. Soon she felt a chill, a need to be warmed.

"Franz, could we possibly have a fire?" she asked as the butler came in to clear the table.

"A fire is set in the morning room, madam. You'll find it lit."

There, settled into a cozy chair, she began to feel more herself. Henry, rapt in silent reflection, stared at the hearth. After a while, he leaned back and began, "I'll tell you about my family. For generations, from Germany to Rumania and far in history to the ancient magicians, they've practiced the art of magic. For centuries they've worshiped the sun, studied the hidden knowledge of old. Fire, you see, is the primal force—the spark and fuel of existence; without it, all would be darkness and death. That is why my forbearers, who called themselves Keepers of the Flame, Masters of Divine Light, have sought from the dawn of civilization to cohere with what they perceived to be the nucleus of life itself."

"The cape! My God, Henry, the colors!"

He nodded gravely. "Black as night without and red as fire within! So it burns, as burns real fire, the cloak of black magic. To walk in the flame without feeling its fury, to make its power one's own, that is the master's art. And more, he searches the annals of subtle knowledge, delving into the depths of philosophy, theology, science. Yet, ever he seeks the same end: to magnify the flame, to become as one with the force that fills all things, seen and unseen. God is light. And light is energy, and fire a form of the same, be it the transformation of this wood we see burning or a mountain to lava or the minutest chemical reaction. That is what my brother believes!"

"Last night ... the fire, the opening of doors, the butler's appearance when Karloff called, yet simultaneous! Could it be?"

"The result of my father's teaching?" He

sighed. "Karloff, you see, is the eldest son. Thus it fell to him to preserve tradition. I too was initiated into the rites of the Order of Divine Light. My mother, alone in her faith, sent me to Vienna at the age of eighteen, determined, it seems, to protect me. Ten years! It's hard to believe."

"This power of which you speak—ability to perform magic or seeming magic—is it dangerous? Or is it merely sleight of hand or some form of hypnotism? I've witnessed such trickery before at traveling shows."

"I would it were so. Remember, when I left this country, I was young with only a young man's knowledge of life. My mother wanted me free of the curse. My parting was in secret. She forbade me to write, lest I be found out." Pausing, he rose and walked to the window. "Perhaps she's there," he mused aloud, "gone to Saint Ann's, the Benedictine Abbey. She often spoke of the place and went on occasion."

"Might we visit and see?"

"I suppose," he said, then continued as though to himself, pacing the room and sitting once more before the fire. "My father, each month when the moon waxed full, I'd see him out by the canyon's edge. There were wolves also that crowded around the circle of light—

the great blaze he'd make in honor of the sun, yet, to these, he was as the fire itself. Though dozens in number, they dared not attack. More than one of their kind had suffered the mark of his anger. Bonfire or none, he could set the whole pack alight if provoked." Again he sighed, searching the flames, lost in a somber realm of distraction.

Muriel, perceiving this, appealed with concern, "Darling, you must forget this past. We have each other. Outside, the sun is shining as in our home. Let us go from this room and these dismal thoughts to the town below or to some pleasant field for a picnic."

"You're probably right. It will do us good to get out. I said so, didn't I? Well then, which would you prefer, town or country?" he asked, standing.

"Town, I think." She smiled.

"Fine! There's a man I'd like to visit, a friend who knows my mother. Maybe he'll have news."

"Splendid!"

"I'll wait in the study. You know your way about, I trust?"

"I won't be long," she assured, kissing him on the cheek.

The study was filled with an impressive

collection of books, in particular those related to the pursuit of human perfection and esoteric knowledge, including the black arts of sorcery and witchcraft. Here, Heinrich, who'd assumed the name Henry on departing for Austria, browsed in search of a volume on the subject of wolves. Remembrance of his father's uncanny ability suggested the subject. And the volume he easily found with like macabre books beginning with W.

"The history of wolves," he read to himself. "Wolves in the wild. Wolves and man. Behavior and habits of wolves. The legend of Romulus and Remus. Wolf anatomy and physiology. The baying of wolves." Here he stopped, reading on about the rapt fascination of wolves with the moon, especially the waxing moon, and their keenness of eyesight and smell in hunting of prey. In the wild, especially in large packs, few animals were equal to their prowess and deadly fangs. Not even a cougar caught and surrounded by a hungry pack was sure to escape. Thus, in a way, the wolf was king of the forest, subject only to the moon at which it bayed. *Might this explain my father's behavior, his desire to subdue and coerce these fearsome mammals? Was this not the aim of the secret Order, to be as the sun in strength and dominion?*

Hearing Muriel approach, he closed the book and returned it to the shelf.

Outside, he was impressed to find the wagon ready and waiting in the drive. How was Franz to know? Could it be Karloff had ordered the vehicle? As they walked up, he saw a note stuck fast to a wooden post with a buck knife. "My brother's doing, no doubt," he assumed aloud. Muriel hesitated, her mind focused on the blade. She shuddered, uncertain of herself, her sudden desire to push the knife deeper into the wood. Taking the note, he read aloud:

> Trust not in the wisdom of fools or gossip of commoners, my brother. Your ride would be easy but for the tides. The ocean afar presses hard on the land; it is felt even here, as is the moon by many a wild thing. Beware, Heinrich! Return before dusk. I warn you!
>
> Karloff

"Surely you must have told him, Henry."

"Quite the contrary. Though it's a fair guess, our being alone and your newness to the area, not to mention my natural inclination to look for Mother."

"But the warning... what can it mean?"

"Idle talk in town that would have us late, I suppose. What difference does it make?"

He was glad to feel the familiar reins and whistled an old German tune as they wound their way down the mountain. When they reached town, it was past noon. Few paid them notice; those who did eyed them with suspicion.

"Lichtenstein!" people whispered. Only the local clockmaker came out to greet the young couple.

"Heinrich Lichtenstein! Why, you're a grown man! Just look at you! And how's this, a young wife? When did you arrive?"

"Yesterday afternoon. We went straight to the castle. Our greeting has been rather cold, I'm sorry to say, apart from your kindness. Muriel, allow me to introduce Jan Schmidt."

"I'm pleased to meet you, Mr. Schmidt!"

"The pleasure is mine to behold such beauty! Heinrich's a lucky man, I see. Come inside, both of you. I've something from Austria to show you."

"Austria! Oh, Henry!"

Going behind a counter, the well-dressed tradesman took out a finely engraved gold pocket watch and laid it before them.

"Magnificent!" Henry exclaimed.

"It's pure gold with the finest detail in every part. Look closely. Examine the gems: rubies, diamonds, emeralds, and sapphires, like so many rays of light in a rainbow. Your mother had me order the watch. She knew you'd return someday. So she left the watch with me for safekeeping. There, take what is yours." Saying this, he sat down on a wooden stool with a feeling of weariness evident to Muriel.

"Can you tell me where she is? I wouldn't ask, but—"

"But you discovered what you feared to be true. Is that it? What did you expect to find? She was wise to have you leave. No, I've told no one. She too has gone, there to Saint Ann's for nigh unto a year. God keep her!"

"Henry, you were right!"

"I would see her, Jan. It's been so many years."

"She's fine, I assure you. I visit there often. But if you must, you'd best get along. There's a two-hour stretch of road to cover."

"Then it seems we'll just have to spend the night. They've room, I trust."

"That they do," he said, rising and escorting them out. "Give her my regards."

"I shall! And thanks for keeping care of this watch. I'll treasure it."

"I'm sure you will."

Henry assisted Muriel into the seat then, mounting the other side, turned to wave. "Good-bye for the present!"

"Good-bye, Mr. Schmidt! I'm glad to have made your acquaintance."

"Safe journey to you both," he bid, looking somewhat concerned, Muriel thought.

They arrived at the convent during afternoon prayer. The sister at the gate was a novitiate. She'd been told by an elder nun—a mentor who'd been suspicious and jealous of Christina ever since her appearance—to say to any who may inquire that no person by the name of Lichtenstein was among their order. This did, in a way, represent the truth, for Christina had come to Saint Ann's seeking refuge. Her concern, however, was only of Karloff, as the nuns were apprised, and not her son Heinrich. Yet, try as he may, his efforts were in vain.

"But surely there's some mistake! I know she's here. I was told by a reputable source, Jan Schmidt of Steinburg, that she came to the abbey not more than a year ago."

"I'm sorry. I have my orders. Perhaps you

might try in the morning and inquire after the Mother Superior. Good day!" she said, closing the window placed in the upper center of the massive door.

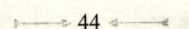

Night of Blood

Evening Entry

It was dusk when Henry and Muriel reached the base of the mountain that rose from the moor to the castle above. They'd entered Steinburg at six o'clock, according to the new watch he'd taken from his waistcoat in front of Jan Schmidt's. But the shop was closed, and he gone out. Muriel yearned to stay, fearing the road. Yet, try as they may, none would have them. "The dread of my family," Henry confessed and so went on, hoping to reach the castle by nightfall.

Muriel's uneasiness grew in invert proportion to the fading light; this she communicated by settling closer to Henry, arms about his waist, as the wagon gathered speed. He too saw the ill omen of a full moon rising in the night sky, its pale glow filtered through branches and felt in each clearing they passed in their harried ascent.

At dark they began, long and clear, bloodcurdling howls that moved in ripples of tension over the horses' flanks. A night owl swooped across the road, causing the team to spook and rear. "Heeyah! Heeyah!" Henry shouted, reigns taut in his hand, whip cracking down at the halted steeds. What he lacked in command the wolves supplied in the strength and proximity of their calls. They'd caught the scent, especially of fear, and rushed like a wind to the sound of wheels and horses. The mares reacted, hastening onward, the owl's spell broken.

Muriel clung tightly to Henry's body, his frame a mass of muscles that strained at their task. He was without fear, a condition that filled him with a new sense of wonder even as he pressed toward the castle. In his astral body, he defied the wolves. "I am master here! This is my land! How dare you invade! How dare you attack! I'll destroy you—all of you—in a moment!" Thus he struggled, his soul divided like unto a man who feels the potential force within yet lacks the wisdom by which to use this awesome might.

At the height of this inner battle, just as the wagon breached the final meadow in view of the castle, they arrived, wave after wave from the east. The race was now of horse and wolf.

No whip was needed to hasten the wild-eyed pair. They flew in a headlong dash of terror, even as the wolves closed in with deadly speed. Seeing the inevitable, Muriel buried her face in Henry's left side while he, buck knife in hand, readied to throw himself at the first beast that approached.

Opposing the challenge, the head wolf flew at man and blade, fangs bared and hair on end. They converged, the knife sinking deep in the vulnerable chest, the fangs in the bloodied arm. Then, all of a sudden, the pack looked aside, a tremendous howl halting its motion. Quickly, Henry bound his wound with a strip of cloth and pulled it tight. Muriel, faint with fear, lay senseless at his side. Again the howl, yet nearer and louder, scattering all but a dozen or more. These were wolves of the southern woods, knowing neither the castle nor its master. Once more the howl, this time high up in a giant elm. Raising their heads, they spied the lone figure. Those wolves that knew moved close to the trees; the rest held fast, intent on the kill. A wolf sprang at the right horse's neck, another at Henry, yet both came short and fell to the ground, each shot through the throat with a single arrow. They'd failed to obey! In a whirl of motion he stood in their midst, his eyes aflame with a seething ire.

Perceiving their prey, the twelve attacked! The sword flashed out with punishing aim, taking an ear, cutting a leg, wounding a chest or side. The great cape lifted. A final howl! They stared in submission at the fire-red wings and man like none they'd ever seen. Now the wolves understood. With yaps and whimpers they eased away, one in wisdom with the rest of the pack. High overhead the moon shone down on the familiar scene, its like dominion also felt by the group that slinked off into the night.

"Why did you fail to heed my words?" the man asked, his back to the wagon. "You who have the same blood in your veins—the purity of race and perfection of form! Yet," he stressed, facing his sibling, "you are wanting in knowledge and skill. Else you'd have no need of my aid. You see this, and still you persist in denial! I'm right, am I not? But come; you are hurt. We'll speak of this later. Now I must take you home."

"Wait! Let me. I should be ashamed were she to awake."

"As you wish! Turn your face aside." A stir of air and rustle of trees followed, then silence.

Drawing Muriel close with his left arm, he

called to the team of horses. They were eager to obey. In moments they reached the castle's main entrance, Franz waiting to lead them into the stables. No mention was made of the incident. Muriel, revived with smelling salts, leaned on Henry's good arm as they made their way to the door. There, at the base of the steps, stood Karloff.

"Heinrich, you're wounded!" he said as though unknowing. "This way; I'll tend to your arm. Franz," he called, "see to the lady's needs. Set a fire in the drawing room and bring her brandy."

"Go, my dear," Henry consented, kissing her forehead. "I won't be long." In mild shock, she pursued the morose butler as directed. When they'd gone, he began. "You are right, Karloff. I too have the blood of our fathers. Had I, as you say, the skill you possess, I'd have braved the wolves in more than will."

"I commend you! For years you've wandered, aimless and ignorant, lost to our line. You, a superior being, born to be ruler of man and nature!"

"And yet we're different, you and I. You think when I speak of defending my own that I'd do as our father—be servant to the black arts? No, Karloff. It's why Mother bade me leave. Why, Father died when he delved too deep, came too close to the fire of which you speak. Or so I assume."

"Were you not injured and partly delirious, I should think you in earnest. But let us desist. You must preserve your strength. Follow me."

The words had the effect of making Heinrich aware of his state: his loss of blood, his need of treatment, and most of all, rest. Moreover, the anger had made his head light and stomach churn. He yielded, the silk cape flowing out before his eyes, and remembered no more.

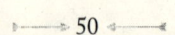

Muriel found herself in a soft leather chair by the fire, the combined effect of her recent trauma and the brandy she'd drunk leaving her hazy and confused. Then, in a flood of anxiety, it came to her: the wolves—the unbearable wolves—the fangs and snarls. "Henry!" she called to the empty chamber. The only reply: an owl's hoot in the night outside. The fire whistled and popped in the hearth. More memories: the lurch of the wagon and strain of the horses, the castle, and Franz. The blood! "Henry, your arm!" Desperate to find him, she hurried out and up to his room, halting at the open door. It was cleaned, the bed neatly made, curtains drawn halfway—not a trace of his things. In a wild frenzy, she threw open the closet, drawers, bathroom; nothing! Overcome by the stress of the day's events, she collapsed.

She awoke to the call of a mockingbird outside her bedroom window and a sharp feeling of hunger pangs. *How did I get here? What can it be?* she wondered. Try as she may, she failed to recall. *Perhaps I've overslept. Henry will be in his room or waiting at breakfast.* Dressing in haste, she went from the chamber to Henry's door. Lifting her hand to knock, she hesitated.

"Madam, I trust you slept well."

"Oh, Franz, what a fright you gave me!" she started with some embarrassment. "Yes, thank you, I slept fine."

"Breakfast is served in the dining room, madam."

"Very good, Franz. I'll be right down."

He nodded, his face livid, and left her alone in the hallway yet waited at the balcony until she began to follow in the direction of the grand staircase. She was relieved in an odd sense that she hadn't knocked, finding more hope in his being at breakfast. What else could the presence of Franz have meant? Retracing her former steps, she passed by the drawing room and came to the dining hall door.

"Come in!" a voice beckoned. She paused,

unsure, both distraught and allured by the sound. He was willing her present, breaking her need to resist. Fighting the urge to flee, she pushed the door open. Her heart sank. The chamber was bare except for Karloff, who stood by the fire, commanding her view. Her head grew light. She would have fainted but for the hand that came out of nowhere and led her forward to a chair. It was he! Yet how? She was seated, water given her to drink. Franz came with a tray laden with food.

"Where is Henry?" she uttered, the fainting spell past.

"Relax, my dear. We Lichtensteins are masters of many arts. And we have here at the castle rooms for every need." His eyes fixed on hers. "You are famished. Eat. I'll come for you later." His words moved in waves of energy, soothed her, caressed her body and soul. All sense of reason was lost to his gaze—his way of reaching her inmost being.

I am yours, she surrendered in silence. *You've won me—brought me to yourself. Whatever you ask, I'll do. I'll do!*

"Good!" he said aloud. "The morning room fire will be lit and ready when you've finished eating." And so he swept from the chamber through a side door. She ate ravenously, reveling in her newfound sensation of desire, intoxicated, alive, exuberant!

Air! I must breathe! Soon, she stood without the main doors, drawing in deeply of the mountain breeze. *The whole world is alive!* She laughed. A chorus of birds echoed her call. She spun in circles, a ballerina doing pirouettes. She touched the blue sky and sunlit clouds. "I'm an angel!" she exclaimed. "A bird soaring on the wind!" Her arms spread out like wings; she glided toward the drive.

"Mother of God! Who is it? What abandon is this?"

Theresa, however, was quick to discern some "evil work," as she noted. The two had just arrived by carriage when they beheld the manic display. "We shall have her right!" she vowed, and stepping forward declared, "Hear me, child! You are in a trance. I break its power in the name of Jesus!" The dancer faltered, like an actress who's forgotten her part. "Jesus sets you free!" the fervent nun imparted, gently laying her hands on the young woman's head then withdrawing them.

"Where ... where am I? Who are you?"

"Be at peace. All is well. Nothing will harm you. I am Sister Theresa from the Convent of Saint Ann. And this is Sister Christina."

"Christina? Henry's mother, of course!" she

affirmed, her relief apparent. "I am Muriel, Henry's fiancée."

Christina marveled. "Forgive me; I'd no idea." She hesitated. "Why, what a surprise!"

"You've something to tell us," Theresa detected.

"It's all been so strange, like a kind of dream. Even now I'm unsure of myself—what's become of him, whether he's well or in some sort of danger. Please, you must help me!"

"Calm yourself. That is why we're here." This she said with a kind of ease, feeling the matter would soon be resolved. "Christina, lead us to where we can sit and visit."

The latter, however, was filled with sudden reserve, being leery of the castle wherein she'd witnessed so much cruelty and death. Yet, what could she do? She too was moved with concern for her son. Into this house she led her companions, the blood chill in her veins, her mind seized with a certain dread—a new conviction that she'd been wrong in coming and bringing her friend, that they'd do better to flee than remain in this realm of horrors.

Trapped

Noon Entry

Henry's eyes opened on a dimly lit room without windows. He lay on an Indian daybed set to one side of the broad, voluminous space. Raising his upper body, he winced, catching his arm with his left hand. The limb, sore throughout to the shoulder and partly swollen at the fore, complained with sharp, biting pain at being so moved. Recalling his former battle with the wolves, he laid back, jaw clenched and eyes pressed tight. Still holding his arm, he examined the space in which he rested. It had, he noticed, the look of a physician's or scientist's lab, with metal and glass instruments arranged methodically on counters and shelves. A skeleton hung from a hook to one side, a large stone slab positioned before it as though the frame of bones was a man observing his victim.

Wanting to view the rest of the room and most of all to stand, he again set his teeth and in one painful move lifted and turned his body. A flush of blood rose to his head. He steadied himself, his whole arm throbbing, and stood, bracing his legs against the bed. The room consisted of several tables, some with chemistry vials, tubes, and like apparatus, others with glass cabinets that held an assortment of dishes and vials filled with various colored liquids. Beyond to the right was a passageway of solid rock lit with torches. Looking round, he saw there was no other exit but for a slender staircase that made its way upward along a curved wall rising off to his left. The stairs, flanked by a sheer edge that dropped thirty feet at its pinnacle to the stone floor, connected high up to another passage.

So this is my father's secret chamber! he perceived. *This is where he performed his experiments.* Conscious of the upper door as a child, he'd dared not enter on account of his mother's stern warnings and the cries and moans he'd heard from without. What had been the source of those voices? He never asked. There was also a complex network running beneath the castle mount—tunnels—partly of nature's and partly of man's doing. He'd explored many of the easier passages reached by means of the upper levels. For the most part, however, he'd kept well away from these hidden regions.

Yet, now his life depended on finding a way out of this prison. He knew that the door of the winding stairs would be locked from without. For Karloff, he grasped in view of his present predicament, had fully assumed the place of their father. The brother he'd known and played with as a child, adventured and explored with as a youth, and looked up to as an elder sibling was no more. The mind that held him captive, in contrast, was not to be trusted.

Meanwhile, in the morning room, Muriel lapsed into a feverish state. "How could I have been so blind and selfish? Why didn't I ask to see him at once?" The nervous display, coupled with her confusion over the night ride and empty bedchamber, made her seem a shaky witness at best to Theresa.

"I understand. Yet, surely it's wise to be patient. For all we know he is safe and well."

"But how?" Muriel struggled, fighting against the specter of Karloff. "I must go this minute to check his room!"

Christina reached out her hand. "I'll go with you. You're in no condition to be alone. Theresa?"

"Fine, if you must. I'll wait for you here."

Muriel neither heard nor remembered the words, her focus on Henry, her fears confirmed by the vacant chamber. By her side, Christina stared in doubt. Then she heard it: the familiar *clap-clap*, the banging of wood, and the fading scream!

"My God! Theresa! Why did I leave her? Hurry; we must run! He knows we are here!" Fleeing to the room from whence they'd come, they froze at the door. There in her place stood Karloff.

"Mother, you've come home; ah, and found my guest, I see. What? Too anxious to wait? I told you, my dear, he rests. Be patient. Sit. How long has it been now, Mother, a year?"

Repelled, Christina knew better than to resist. The words were but a thin veneer that hid a vast chasm of arrogant pride. She must play her part, as before, in this terrible drama or become his next victim. "Karloff, you are here," she said with concealed effort, obeying his wish and sitting with Muriel on a sofa. He stood to the left of the fireplace, hand on the mantle, facing them at an angle.

"You're spry, Mother, I see. Though I should think life in a cloister the surest way to weaken a body." This he said with contempt, as though it were simple scientific fact and those who failed to admit the truth were of no consequence.

"God is gracious, my son."

"What god? A god who gives blood to drink, floods the world, and walks on water? And who, as you say, is so weak as to let himself be nailed to a piece of wood. Foolish woman you are!" As he spoke, his eyes flashed, the dark brows narrowed in a look of disdain.

"Please, do not blaspheme. I beg you!"

"Father warned me about your vain superstitions," he countered, ignoring her plea. "I won't allow it, this idle dream of fools who constitute the common mass of lesser men and feeble women!"

"Like Sister Theresa?" she asked, reading his thoughts.

He smiled within at their mutual gift, the uncanny ability that came from her family who, like the Lichtensteins, were of traveling gypsy and soothsayer stock. "As you say, Mother," he replied, suggesting it was she and not he who'd caused the presumptuous nun's removal and shifting as he spoke to stand before the fire.

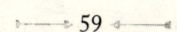

Muriel, Christina noticed with alarm, was relapsing into her former trance, her eyes trained on Karloff's head, her body erect and stiff. "Karloff, what have you done?" she pleaded. "Where have you taken her?"

"Why don't you inquire of your god?" he mocked. "The one who has made the world, the sun, moon, and stars, the wolves that hunt in the night, howling at the sky? No, Mother, you are wrong! It is I, Karloff, who saved your beloved Heinrich from the hungry pack. And I who'll save you from a worse fate, yet, pining away, as you are in a senseless abbey."

"But, you wouldn't—"

"Harm him? Do you think I'd spare him, merely to extend his miserable life in some foreign city? Heinrich is come, as I knew he would. He is destined to keep the flame—the fire that fills and devours all things! Though you have sought to prevent him!"

"But, Sister Theresa! Surely you wouldn't harm her?"

"She's of no consequence." He looked aside. "If god, as you presume to believe, is with her, then he will protect her." Thus saying, he lifted his cape and spun about, masking the flames in a cover of black then coming full circle, arms lowered, eyes gleaming in triumph. The fire was out! Christina perceived the will of her son.

"We'll go to our rooms," she yielded, knowing the discussion was over.

"As you wish. Trouble me not till evening!"

Standing with Muriel, she took a few steps and looked back. No one! *Oh, Theresa, what have I done? What has become of you?* Just then, Franz came out.

"Madam,"—he nodded gravely—"the master bids me escort you upstairs."

While he spoke, Theresa waded in a subterranean pool. She was near to where Christina now stood when her hands flew upward as her body slid down and through a smooth wooden shoot that emptied into a deep water cavern. As her feet touched bottom and legs pushed upward, she noticed a bright hole in the rock wall that separated the pool into which she'd plunged from a further volume of water. Having descended twice to the narrow portal, drawn by the promise of escape from her dark cell, she'd failed to get past on account of her garments.

"Heavenly Father," she pleaded when the confinement of space grew unbearable, "please show me the way. Help me, Lord! What am I to do?" In answer, a scripture came to her mind: "It is easier for a camel to go through the eye of a needle than for a rich man to enter the kingdom of God."

What can it mean? she asked herself. *I've left everything. I've nothing to give—no riches.* Then it hit her—the loss of her father at sea, her mother's grief and fear, her own decision to join the convent instead of pursuing her father's call. *To be a missionary!* she realized—the dream of her youth.

"Oh, Lord, I've been blind! I chose the protection of a cloister, hid behind these habits. But how can I put them off to my shame?" Verses came in a flood of memory, scriptures she'd taken to heart as a child, her soul filled with missionary zeal. Tears came too, fast and hard, falling in a steady stream that merged with the silent pool. In a rush of exuberant resolve, she stripped from her garments, feeling the freedom of being released.

Into the silky water she plunged, her soft cotton underskirt close on her skin. Reaching her hands toward the glimmer ahead, she straightened and angled to the side, aligning herself with the slender passage. First arms, then chest, abdomen, hips, legs. She was out and kicking her way to the surface. Her head broke through into the light, water rippling away in rings, cool air filling her lungs. The cavern was large, with a door to the side. *It must be ten feet up,* she estimated. Yet, seeing this to be the only exit, she swam over to the wall and searched its surface, feeling for cracks and crevices. No use. The wall was flat and slick to the touch.

Soon she heard footsteps, first faint, then louder as though approaching. She pressed against the rock. Luckily, her foot found a gap, allowing her to embrace the wall. The steps halted. A hand grasped the edge of the portal above. She trembled with fear, feeling almost ashamed. The hand withdrew, and steps resumed.

"Wait!" She panicked, cognizant of her plight. The steps quickened, and soon a face peered into the cavern, a man she'd never seen. He looked about in awe, yet finding no one would have left when the voice came again. "Here below!"

"What in God's name? How came you there? No matter. I'll get some rope. Can you hold on?"

"Yes," she replied, "I'll manage."

He returned in minutes and what seemed with great effort, the rope about his waist, pulled her up and out, supporting her at the last with his left arm and shoulder. She was, he thought, the most beautiful woman he'd ever seen. And she, ignorant of her own loveliness, blushed in response to his attention.

"You're wet," he said, collecting his wits. "Wait here! I'll search for a towel."

"And some clothing," she suggested, sensing his earnest.

"Of course. Forgive me. I am Henry," he offered. "And you would be?"

"Theresa," she replied, unable to add the word *sister*.

"Please," he asked, raising his hand in a posture of wait and leaving on his promised errand. She in turn put her back to the side of what appeared to be a tunnel or natural cave, discretely mindful of her visible figure.

Finding the door open as he'd left it, he searched for the desired items in the anteroom of the great chamber.

"You want to escape, Heinrich?" Karloff emerged from the long, arched passage connecting the rooms.

"I want an explanation!" he retorted, emboldened by his brother's presumption.

"Explanation? You waste your life on petty knowledge gleaned from the works of common men! You fled on a whim, a woman's emotion. You who were meant to direct!"

"What of our father? I see no honor in his death or the practice of magic—the curse of our family!"

"Beware what you say! You know little of truth—the real answers you seek; for this I forbear you."

"What would you do? Force me to follow? Bind me, with you, to the fate of our fathers! When will it end?"

"You speak as a novice, as one who's stifled by base affairs, vain pursuits of vulgar men untaught in the power that rules all things!"

"I would know this: why our father made waste of innocent lives in this den of horror, why you tread so close in his path! You've mastered the secret arts, I gather. He, no doubt, taught you well. What, then, will you also destroy in the name of science? Will you—"

"Silence! No more of your words! Tomorrow, when the sun is at its peak, you will choose either to learn the way of the Order and become a Keeper of the Flame or to wander the caves till you perish with hunger. There is no way out. I alone have the key to the upper door. Think well, my brother!"

"But Muriel, my fiancée! And Mother!"

"They are here and unharmed. Be ready at noon!" With that, his cape floating behind him, he merged with the tunnel and was lost to sight.

"What's the use? Damn him!" Henry swore. Finding a flint and knife, along with some cord that fit his pocket and a candle, he retraced his steps. The flicker of light made Theresa stand with relief. "I'm sorry. It's this bloody castle! We're trapped, it would seem. I double-checked the door above—locked from without; my dear brother's doing. And I've nothing to bring. There wasn't a towel or piece of clothing anywhere," he said in frustration.

"Then we'll make a way," she determined, stirred by his speech. "We are here. You have found me I cannot believe without cause."

Such beauty and realism! "You are right," he acknowledged. Yet, what could he offer? Pointing, he explained, "This way leads to a hole in the canyon's side. It's a direct plummet, a hundred feet or so, to the river."

"And that way?"

"A maze of tunnels running beneath and away from the castle. I learned of them as a boy. The ones higher up I know, yet these I've never explored."

"What of the river? It flows to the east of Steinburg, through the canyon. We can see it from Saint Ann's."

"That's the one, all right! Comes down from the mountains in countless streams. The water will be high from the late spring run-off and mighty deep. If I could just force the door at the top of the steps! But it's no use. I've tried and searched for a key; there's only one, and Karloff has it."

"Could we reason with him, make him see his error?"

"Apparently you don't know him. Who do you suppose sent you into the cavern? Good thing I was here! No, I fear he's beyond our reach."

"No one's beyond the reach of God."

"Maybe so. All the same, I don't care to risk my life, or yours, on such a notion. He refuses to listen! We, therefore, have but one option: explore the caves in hope of finding a way out of this maze."

"The river, you say it's deep."

"Deep as a mountain lake in spots, when the water's up. Surely you don't mean?"

"What real choice have we? Stay here and wait in fear and doubt as I've done so long? Or jump and trust our lives to God! The caves seem hardly reliable from what you've said."

Once again, he marveled at her words. Muriel would not have conceived such a plan in a hundred years. No, she wasn't brave, merely intrigued by the foreign and mysterious. It had, he reflected, been her desire to visit that decided their trip to the castle to begin with. But here, here was a woman like him—strong, courageous, practical.

"Perhaps you might first consider the nature of what you propose," he suggested. "This way." They went, hand in hand, to the large portal that shone before them around two bends in the tunnel. "Hold firm to my hand!" She reeled back, dazed by the sight. "Not so easy, I think." He laughed.

"The cliff is straight and the water smooth," she indicated, finding her courage.

"You amaze me! I should think you an angel sent to lead me from prison."

"What angel would be caught in a pool as I was?"

"Whatever the case, our fate is apparent: to leave this spot with small chance of survival."

"Here, I must differ. I may have cloistered myself in a convent, but there I learned much of God's ways. Do you think he'd allow me to live and bring you to my aid for no reason?"

"If only I had your faith; mine has been sorely tested these past days. And my arm is weak from its wound. Yet, what is that?" Taking her hands, he looked in her eyes.

"Together!" she affirmed, needing his strength.

"Right!" He nodded. "We jump together, hard and fast, and pray to God the water is deep; if it is, it'll be a ways back up to the surface, mind you, and the current will carry us forward."

"I understand." She readied, feeling the support of his hands and easing with him to the edge of the opening. "Oh God," she prayed, "make us able. Guide us safely down and bring us up whole and unharmed." Before she had time to say "Amen," an eagle swooped down and hovered in the wind straight out from the cave; with a cry, it dove! The wall of fear broken, they followed in unison, hands held firm, spirits joined as one.

Dark Bride

Night Entry

Standing before an open window, Christina watched as an eagle circled above and beyond the canyon ridge; it hovered a while then dropped out of sight. Moments later she heard its cry, then others—human cries—faint but clear that echoed across the canyon.

What on earth? She trembled, her mind racing, searching for an answer. *The caves!* she apprehended. *The holes in the canyon wall!* "Oh, Heinrich, Heinrich!" she called out in despair, weeping into her hands. No reply, but a knock at the door. She lifted her head, and there before her perched on the ledge sat a female dove. Again the knock, this time sending the dove up and away. Wiping her eyes, she went to the door.

"Are you all right, madam?"

"Yes, Franz, I believe so," she replied, viewing the dove as a sign from heaven.

"Can I get you anything?"

"Really, I'm fine. It's just, I thought I heard…"

"Madam?"

"Oh, I don't know. I might have imagined," she said, rather distractedly. "But then, the dove."

"Dove, my lady?"

"Silly, I know. Yet a dove came here at the window. And when I saw it, the voices lightened."

"Lightened?" he pursued.

"Receded. I feel they are safe, though I can't say how."

"That is well, my lady," he said, accepting her explanation without need of reason. "Might I prepare some lunch?" This he suggested with an air of familiarity, like one freed from restrains, if only for a brief interval. He was, she knew, her late husband's cousin, come from the old country twelve years past and asked to remain as butler. A simple man, he soon learned the ways of the house and fulfilled his duties without complaint. He, like her, was a kind of prisoner, playing an endless game of charades.

"Thank you, Franz; that would be most welcome." Bowing in silence, he departed down the hall and out of sight. Just then, laughter caught her ear. She moved to Muriel's door and touched the knob; it was locked, a skeleton key left for her use. *Franz!* she thought. *He must have heard.*

"Muriel!" She knocked. No answer. She waited. Again, the laughter and sounds of movement. Bracing herself, she turned the key. The curtains were closed and the occupant sprawled out wide on the bed, her arms and legs outstretched as though strapped with cords to the corner posts.

"Henry!" she pleaded, straining against her invisible bands. "Henry! Henry!" Her eyes were wild and set in a fixed sort of passion.

"Muriel, it's me, Christina! Can you hear me?" Her words brought no answer.

"I'm yours, Henry! All of me! Hold me! Love me!" she begged, casting her body side to side.

Somehow the action reminded Christina—the wild dancing and hysterics without the castle, Theresa's reaction, the release of Muriel from her trance. In a desperate effort, she was at the bedside, uttering the prayer she'd heard, touching the girl's head. "Thank God!" she sighed as Muriel grew limp and quiet. She covered her up with a blanket.

"What's happened?"

"Be calm, child. Rest a bit."

"But Henry, he was here!"

"Get dressed when you're ready," she encouraged, glancing out the window. "I'll wait for you in the hall." Closing the door behind her, she went to a chair by the upper balcony in view of the grand stairs and main entry. *He knows I'll stay, that I won't leave without her. Surely they've gone, somehow escaped! Those cries! But Theresa; is it possible? Am I to believe?* So ran her thoughts, all the while centered on Muriel and what they must do. She stood and went back to the door; it was open and Muriel departed!

She was, that instant, broaching a passage that wound its way upward into a tower, the effect of the trance clouding her mind, making Henry and Karloff one and the same. *He's here,* she sensed, gripping the banister that curled around like a giant snake. *I must find him!* At last she reached a slender, arched door and stopped, catching her breath, her body electric with shrill excitement. From behind, Christina's voice called out, hushed, doubtful, as though dreading the passage. Her steps came closer. In a panic, Muriel turned the handle and pushed.

A shaft of light hit her head-on and caused

her to blink and squint into the surrounding darkness. She stood within a circular space, a round window in the ceiling above leading her eye to a prostrate figure that lay, draped in black, in the room's center. A hand closed over her mouth, a second hand grasping her arm. She froze in terror. For there, before her, was a face pale as death, the eyes open wide—bright, red eyes trained on the sky. It was Karloff, his body motionless, rigid as a corpse. Yet no bed or structure supported his frame. He floated in air, like a phantom bat, stark and forbidding.

Slowly, carefully, Christina eased her from the room, closing the door without a sound. "Hurry," she urged, "we must leave before he revives."

"But... but how...?"

"There's no time. Be quiet for your life!" So, descending the tower, they came to the exit and fled through the halls to the stairway and thence the main doors and drive without. "Quick, the carriage! We have to make haste!"

"But Henry! How can I?"

"He's left! Trust me. I can't explain. Please, Karloff is coming!"

Muriel looked at the castle. "How can I?" she repeated and ran for the door.

"Muriel, wait!" Her call was ignored. And

search as she may, no trace of the girl. "Merciful heavens, he has her! Please, someone!"

In response, the butler appeared, his eyes alight. "Madam, you called."

What could she do? She must tell him everything. "Franz," she began, "how long have I known you?"

"Twelve years, my lady."

"And in that time have you never been troubled by things you've seen or talk in the town?"

"I try not to be. But yes, I hear rumors."

"Yet you see no cause?"

"I see only my duty."

"You needn't pretend. I know the truth—the sins of my husband, the state of my son. And I know you have loved me, wished me happy. It's why I left. For Karloff, he wouldn't allow such kindness."

"I'm your servant, my lady. Whatever you ask, I'll do."

"We'll do together," she prompted. "Heinrich's fiancée has vanished like the others. Help me find her. I fear she's trapped somewhere below. You know the way, Franz?"

"To all but the secret room, madam. It is locked. And Karloff has warned me never to enter should I find it open."

"And here in the floor, the trap doors! You know of these too?"

"Such doors are common in large estates; they are generally used in case of burglars or those who seek to do harm."

"But here! Have you ever seen them used?"

"No, my lady, never."

"Well, then let us see what awaits beneath these dreadful floors." They went, as she wished, together through a side door in the parlor to which he had a key and from whence a corridor led to a wooden staircase that spiraled downward and opened at various levels below. The way was familiar to lady and butler, though neither had been there often, and both had rather be elsewhere.

"Here we are," he whispered, "the lowest level. The door I believe is past the turn in the wall."

"Listen, Franz! Do you hear? The voice!"

"You are right." He swallowed, his neck hair on end. "I am not so bold," he apologized. "I'll wait for you above." He shook like a man who's seen a ghost and became insensible, fleeing up the stairs to the light of day, leaving only a candle behind.

She too might have fled were it not for her pained sympathy with Muriel's plight.

Rounding the bend, she noticed a streak of yellow light on the passage floor. The door was ajar, awaiting her entry. Candlelight danced on the wall ahead as she passed through the tunnel and neared the top step. Muriel's cries were now sharp in her ears, plaintive, yearning, filled with agony of desire, expectation. She could bear it no longer! Down she went, the wall dropping off to her left where Muriel lay on a great stone table, hands and feet fastened with leather thongs.

"Ah, Mother, at last! I've been waiting." Karloff stepped from a tunnel and stood by his captive, who ceased to struggle when he approached. "It is you I must thank for this vessel," he said, his hand passing over Muriel's face.

"What can you mean?"

"Mean? She will have a son, a master who'll take my place—a Lichtenstein!"

"I beg you no! You mustn't!"

"I shall! He has spurned my will, despised his duty! I'm done with him! Here, I'll keep what is mine."

"I won't listen, neither believe she is yours! I have prayed for you, son. And yet you persist in this evil, this work of your father."

"The words of a woman, weak and unstable.

There is only life, and life is power—power to create and destroy, power to give life, as I shall do. You are blind to what I have seen. Be gone! Keep your prayers. The line must endure!"

"But this girl, she hasn't given herself, not to you!"

In a flash, a knife shone out. The bands were cut. A line of blood emerged from his arm. The girl, seeing it, threw herself forward like a wild beast, clasping the arm with either hand. She caught the stream before it dropped then made her way to the main source, licking her lips as she pressed the flesh as if to bring a faster flow.

"Oh God!" Christina gasped, her back to the wall, her stomach wrenching at the sight. The girl sucked on till the blood ran dry then lifted her face, teeth and lips dripping, and smiled with pleasure.

He raised his arm and pointed to the upper portal. Stricken with horror and grief, she fled, mourning Muriel's fate. For a moment she wavered. A hand caught her shoulder.

"No, my lady!"

"Oh, Franz," she sobbed. "How can I leave her?" It wasn't his concern, having come for her safety, but only to depart once more in haste. They went to the spiral stairs and ascended.

"The carriage is ready and waiting, madam." They'd reached the parlor door. "We must go at once!" Beside herself with sorrow, she yielded, grateful for his aid. "I shall take you to the convent," he said, assisting her to the velvet seat then closing the door. His words faded.

She recovered to the lurch of the coach as it moved, leaving behind the dungeon and prey. It was late afternoon when they came to Saint Ann's. But where was Theresa? Had she jumped to the river with Heinrich? Or were they yet captive, lost somewhere in the castle labyrinth?

"Sister Christina! What's become of Sister Theresa?"

"I don't know," she admitted, tears flowing down her face.

"Come with me. We'll go to Mother Superior."

"Wait,"—she paused—"Franz, you'll stay with Jan Schmidt, as agreed. Don't dare venture back! Promise me!"

"I promise." He bowed. She watched as he maneuvered the vehicle and gently whipped the team into action.

Inside, she walked with her fellow novitiate across the familiar paths and corridors of the abbey, stopping before the main office as her companion knocked and departed.

"Come in!" a voice beckoned. It was Sister Ann. She'd been in prayer with the Reverend Mother since noon, neither having taken food.

"Tell us, child," Mother Germane asked, her face lined with care, "whatever you can. We feel in our spirits Theresa's in danger."

Her reply made evident their concern. They'd heard many ill accounts of the castle. Yet, the past years had been without incident, save for the coming of Christina—the novitiate who now shed tears of remorse in the wake of her trial.

"I am to blame," her superior confessed. "I should never have let you go in the first place. However, like you, we trust she's alive."

"The journey by foot would take almost two days," Sister Ann estimated. "If they survived the fall Christina described, they could be here by evening tomorrow."

"And if harmed, they'll need our care," the elder nun added with a distant look. "Rest from your journey. Abstain from food till morning if you can. I'll expect you at vespers."

"Thank you, Mother." She bowed.

"Let us hope, come tomorrow, our prayers will be answered."

Survival

Dawn Entry

Riding a current of air with outstretched wings, a great blue heron followed the stream in its southerly course. The sun slipped over the western mountains. Below, by the bank, a man thrust a sharp-ended pole into the river. The spear he'd made from a branch, using his knife to sharpen the end. This time he felt the thrash of a large fish excite the primitive instrument. Lifting the spear straight up and back, he laughed at the sight of a mammoth trout, result of an hour's labor.

"Theresa!" he shouted. Coming from a thicket with an armload of wood, she took in the vision of hunter and fish, reflecting his pride with a radiant smile.

"That's splendid, Henry!" she heard herself say. He'd held her hand as they fell, found her above water, and brought her to the riverbank downstream. They'd walked for hours in the warm sun, stopping to make camp when she grew tired. He'd fashioned a spear and caught a fish. He would protect her through the long night. She laid out the dry sticks with the other wood she'd collected and went to gather tall grass with which to make beds.

Henry, gutting and cleaning the trout, busied himself with a flint, fanning into flame the sparks. The fire spread quickly from grass to brush and wood. For a moment, the specter of Lichtenstein castle rose before him. He thought of Muriel and his mother, there alone. Were they safe? Had they made an escape, perhaps with Franz? Theresa returned, laden with grass.

"A fire! How nice!"

"Won't be fancy,"—he shrugged—"a lone trout cooked on a rock. But I think we'll have our fill."

"And a place to rest."

"So I see." She delighted, allured him, made him wish he were Adam and she his Eve, that all his life had been a dream and she the only reality, measure, and true completion of himself. Was this her doing? No, she was discretion itself, solely concerned for his and Muriel's good. The realization made him sensible, somewhat ashamed of his attraction.

They ate in silence, cleaning the bones,

neither feeling a need to speak. A soft wind rustled in the trees. The fire danced, and out beyond the river flowed with quiet strength. Seeing the impressive skeleton laid out on the flat-topped rock that served for their table, she was suddenly conscious. Never had she eaten so freely. It was almost sinful, she thought. Yet, she didn't care. He was there. They were one in need and fulfillment. She looked happy and pleased—all he desired.

They sat and visited into the evening, two fellow beings that together escaped the hand of death and braved a day of hardship. They opened to each other, baring their souls in a way that neither dreamed possible. Slowly, painfully the patterns of their lives unfolded, gaining added meaning in the course of conversation. Daylight faded. Stars grew bright.

"We'll sleep well tonight," he said, adding wood to the blaze. "The canyon is steep for miles in either direction. No animals are apt to bother us here. I'll tend to the fire."

Assured by his words, exhausted and grateful, she left his side and settled into her grassy bed, her prayers fading into a profound rest. He came after, gently covering her with his jacket, and soon gave way to sleep, waking twice in the night when the flame grew dim. Up before dawn, he again stoked the fire, adding more wood till a warm glow illumined the camp. For a while he sat and looked at her face, the light playing over her classic features. He gazed downriver. They'd have to move on by land or water till the canyon's height and severity lessened as it did to the east of Steinburg.

"Henry?" a soft voice searched.

"Go back to sleep. We've a long day ahead."

"What about you?"

"I'll be fine; don't worry. Get your rest; you'll need it." Feeling the warmth of the fire, she closed her eyes.

Come sunrise over the canyon they were well downstream, having found a thicket of berries en route that served as meager fare. By midday, they'd crossed the river twice, floating on makeshift rafts he made out of driftwood fastened in place with a cord of rope. The water widened, the forest above to the west giving way to open country. They considered the current.

"We're approaching a parallel point to town."

"What can we do?"

"We'll have to brave the rapids; no other way. The cliff's too steep upstream." She nodded, helping him ready a rig and wading with him in the water. "Here, put your arm around my waist; hang on to the raft with the other. I'm not about to lose you!" Once more, they pushed out into the river. "Kick," he shouted against the roar, "hard as you can!" They struggled through the rush of water, the raft angled toward the far side. More than once they went under, guiding their bark around huge boulders. With great effort they reached the center, the channel deep and free of obstacles.

"Henry, I can't make it!"

"Hold on! Hold to me!" he yelled, his protective anger giving her strength. She kicked. The raft edged forward across the center to the far rapids. It was the supreme test—more boulders forcing them round and under, their raft being swept along by the stream. Up ahead, a long tree trunk, fallen and fixed over part of the river, came into view.

"Look!" She panicked.

"Reach when I say! Whatever you do, hold fast to me!" His muscles tensed. The trunk was upon them! "Reach!" His hands clung to the solid wood.

"Henry, I'm slipping!"

In a second he had her, adrenaline shooting through his veins. "Put your arm around my neck! That's it! Now get on my back!" As she did, his left hand grasped the branch. Inch by inch, he maneuvered the limb, every part of his body alive. Only when his feet touched bottom did he let go. They were safe! Wading to shore, they threw themselves into each other's arms; then, taking hands, they walked over the pebbled beach and up a gentle slope to the mainland. Finding a soft place in the grass, they reclined and took in the clear blue sky. The sun was warm, the air fragrant, the earth a bed on which they lay: their Eden restored, if but for an hour. Would God, the time might last forever! It couldn't be. They must venture on, be carried by the stream of life, not back but forward. She to the world of missions, and he...?

"Ready?" he asked reluctantly.

"Yes. It's just that I—"

"You needn't say. We've had quite a ride. I'll never forget."

"Forget?" she pursued.

"The whole journey, I'd say." He wanted to say *you*. She shared his desire, the conflict of feelings, of internal and external realities—his engagement, her missionary vow, still a secret. Taking hands, they stood and made their way west across the moor to town and the welcoming wave of Franz.

"What wonder is this, Franz?"

"My lady Christina, sir, she bid me wait."

"Ah, thank God! But how did she know?"

"That I can't say, sir."

"Never mind. A woman's intuition, I suppose. We're here, as you see, yet famished!"

"I shopped this morning, sir. I'll prepare something directly."

"Excellent! Ah, Jan, how are you, my friend?"

Jan, hearing the voices, had come to the yard from the kitchen door. "Better than you from the look of things."

"Good-natured as always!" Henry laughed, taking his hand. "Jan, this is Theresa, a sister from Saint Ann's."

"Follow me, young lady. I'll find you some clothes to tide you over." He motioned, perceiving her unspoken need. "Then we shall eat, and you can tell me all your adventures." The words were a pleasant welcome, and soon they found themselves at the table enjoying a proper feast prepared by the diligent butler. Food had never tasted so good. And Jan marveled as they finished the various courses. "I'm honored by your appetites. Maybe I'll ask your Franz to stay."

Henry smiled. "We're most grateful! We've had little enough these past two days."

"I appreciate the clothes," Theresa added.

"For such company and stories, my door is open any time, I assure you," he pledged with the same warm humor.

"Now, it seems, we have to be on our way."

"What a shame! Well, you must come again, and soon. Do say hello to Christina. Such a prize watch she's given you!" he reflected.

"The watch! I'd almost forgotten." He pulled the timepiece out of his pocket. "A bit worse for wear, I'm afraid."

They stood from the table, the craftsman taking the item from his outstretched hand. "I see," he replied, looking the instrument over. "Fortunately, it can be repaired, though I may need parts from Vienna."

"Ah, that's a relief!"

"Not a word to your mother, hear. I'll have it right with some work."

"How grand! I thank you again!"

"Yes, thanks for everything!"

"Spoken by a rare beauty," he said with a twinkle and side glance at Heinrich.

"You are too kind." She smiled.

"And you will be late. Franz, I think, is impatient."

"He's a singular fellow," Henry admitted, escorting Theresa through the front door to the carriage without where Franz sat waiting. "Good-bye for the present."

"Farewell to you both!" With that, they were off to Saint Ann's. They'd make it by dusk, to the shared relief of the nuns, especially Christina, who wept on her son's arm.

"All can be explained in the morning," Mother Germane determined, seeing the travelers' need of rest. "Sister Ann, show the men to the guest rooms. Everyone else to bed! The bell is ringing!"

Dance of Death

Afternoon Entry

Henry sat with his head inclined to the north and vision cast through a tall, pointed, arch-framed window to a sky massed with stars that carried his thoughts from Theresa, fast asleep in another room, to the journey they'd taken and from thence to the caverns and secret chamber of the distant castle. "Muriel," he spoke to the night air. He knew nothing of her real trials, his late arrival preventing time with his mother. *I'll ask in the morning,* he resolved, too tired to think.

"Muriel!" he called out amidst the fog, moving across the yard toward the castle. A pale moon hung overhead, its bleak light bathing a figure high atop the roof. It was her he saw. A man appeared, coming from behind, his cape extended and closing around her in a veil of blackness. The arms flew outward. She was gone! Only the phantom of red remained. "Muriel, no!" he lamented, perceiving her fate.

The phantom leapt to the precipice, ready to swoop down. Suddenly it reeled, turned back in alarm, and fell in a tangle of red and black. Fire sprung from the castle! All was alight! And there, swaying in confusion at the roof's edge, stood Muriel. "Wait!" he cried and ran to the main door, passing through fire and smoke to the housetop. Throwing his body against the door, he awoke!

The day was cold and lowering, the sun lost behind a cover of clouds. *A bad omen*, he thought, recalling his dream. Nor in body did he wish to make the trip. Still, he'd no choice.

"But you can't go alone! Please, son!"

"She's right," Mother Germane agreed. "From all you and Sister Theresa have told us, it's far too dangerous."

"Very well; if you insist, I'll speak with Jan Schmidt. Perhaps he can find some willing men."

"That will be wise."

"Many, I regret to say, have suffered the curse of our family. Far too long has its shadow been on the land."

"You were safe in Vienna. Why, Heinrich, did you not stay? To lose you now… I cannot bear it!"

"Mother, I must! The news of father's death,

then Muriel's desire to visit, and Karloff…" He stopped in anger. "I'll never understand him!"

"Nor could you," the senior nun asserted. "Yet, one thing's clear: God has preserved your life for a purpose."

"You sound like Theresa."

"Trust in his will! Rely on his strength! Our prayers are with you."

"I appreciate it; thank you!"

Soon he was at the carriage. He bid his mother good-bye and signaled. Franz, waiting, cracked the whip.

In Steinburg, the call went out for volunteers. Few were willing to brave the castle. Too many deaths and dreadful accounts—bone-chilling stories of wandering vagrants cut to pieces and hung from the canyon wall or thrown, half-alive, to the river below. And always the same when officials went out to investigate—the bodies gone, vanished without a trace! None approached the place at dusk but those who'd known the former master—men from afar who ate at his table in raucous feasts and unruly locals who lived out of town. Then there were his sons—one thought to be the baron himself revived from the grave, the other departed years past, now returned as a meddler asking for aid.

"They're all I could muster," the clockmaker owned, three men by his side. "I too would go, but I've work to do on your watch, young Heinrich, seeing you might depart before long."

"I'm obliged," he acknowledged, shaking the men's hands.

"There's the devil himself behind those walls!" Hans Beckner contended. "You'll pardon my saying so."

"Pardon or no, it's fact!" Jan Kohlberg stressed.

"I'm with you, men," the local smithy, Sven Dyke, put in. "That mansion is evil! I'd as soon stay, but for the town's sake."

"Two days ago I might have questioned your words. I came in hope of reaching out to Karloff, my brother. I fear, however, he's completely given to my father's conduct. Yet, may I remind you of our purpose: to rescue my fiancée, Muriel, and get her safely away. If you've other business, it will be to you, though I warn you against provocation. That is my counsel."

"What do you suggest?" Jan asked.

"Stay well behind the carriage on horseback. Wait and watch from the woods that border the grounds to the south. Approach only on signal from Franz or myself; when you do, come as guests, as though invited by me. Should I meet with resistance, your presence will be vital to my goal. Otherwise, use your judgment."

"That's well spoken, I'd say," the smithy approved.

"Let's get our horses." Jan nodded. Soon they were saddled and on the road, the carriage ahead crossing the moor.

In Muriel's mind, he was with her—her beloved fiancé and husband—had been there all along in the castle, the home she'd wandered through hour upon hour. He'd captured her soul, ravished her heart, entered her body in sacred union. They'd become as one. She walked in a dream, troubled only at times when she felt his absence. She'd search and search, but always the same: empty rooms and corridors, a fire inviting her to stay in this or that chamber. Then he'd be there, a flame in his eyes. They'd eat or make love, and he would depart. She'd come out of need, drawn by the threads of his past, thrilled by the castle that grew in her mind (had grown in her mind as they traveled from Vienna) and closed her into its silent world.

"I'm a butterfly!" she mused, fluttered before an upper window, floating and whirling as on the breeze. Then came the sound, the rattle of wheels. Her thoughts wandered. Once more she rode in the carriage at Henry's side, rounding the bend that revealed his home. The same feeling of dread and excitement caused her to cease in the dance and move to the window. The carriage was as she remembered, its horses sleek and sable brown. And there sat Henry. "Henry?" she faltered, her mind confused. He stood before her, face intent.

"Go to your room. I've business!" He shut the window and looked in her eyes. "You are tired," he said. She felt the phrase deplete her energy.

"I am tired, my love, so tired." He made no reply but turned and left. Tracing the upper hall with her fingers, she found the bedroom and closed the door.

"Wait here, Franz. Be ready to signal the others. He isn't likely to challenge me in the open, not in your view. Keep to our plan."

"As you wish, sir."

In Henry's estimation, Karloff had broken all bonds of affection. He wasn't the brother he'd known but a servant of secret arts practiced by few who dared hazard the path of divine light—the fire that consumed their father and the force that Karloff had learned to use to ignoble ends.

He searched the front windows; all were closed, and the form he'd seen was nowhere in sight. The fog thickened, rolling in waves before and around him.

"Why have you come, Heinrich?"

The voice was Karloff's, yet, looking upward, he saw no one. "Where are you? Show yourself!"

"You were careful at first to bring me an offering. She will have a child. And unlike you, he'll honor the memory of our father's."

"Our father is dead, destroyed, I assume, by the sorcerer's flame. Are you to be next?"

"What death, my brother? There is only the light—the way of dominion, wisdom, and power you've chosen to spurn. Will you never cease to try my patience?"

The words he discerned came from above, high on the rooftop. Then he saw her, a picture of confusion! She'd come to a window; it was open! She could hear him! He perceived the opportunity even as he read her countenance. "You confess it all, Karloff—father's wrongdoing, your taking of Muriel, my fiancée. Tell me, how did you convince her once you'd locked me in the dungeon, forced me to jump from the cliff to the river?"

"There you are wrong! You jumped on your own. To me she surrendered, even before you left your precious Vienna."

She was moving, holding her head, rocking from side to side. "Are you sure, Karloff? Rather, I see she's been deceived."

At this, even as she withdrew from the window, he came forward and glared down at his impudent sibling. "You dare to go on, to test me further? Be gone, or your life will end!" He stood poised on the edge, ready to fly in anger. Then his head lifted, and he looked to the south.

Henry stepped back. He too heard the voice—their mother's plea. Too late! The knife! A hideous scream! Two figures locked in a dance of death! A cloud of mist obscured his vision. They fell in a wild flurry of color, the cold earth waiting in silence below.

"No!" Henry moaned, his knees giving way in sudden despair, his head hung low, eyes blinded by tears. Slowly, he stood, the bodies draped in a cloak before him all he could see through the shifting fog. A blaze of light and then another halted his approach and attracted his focus to the castle. The fire spread swiftly, room to room, as though urged on by a vengeful hand.

He threw himself at the velvet cape, grasping the shoulder and pulling in doubt. A shock sent him reeling away in horror. *What on earth? My God!* Franz and the others came up from the drive as he ran to the door. "Muriel!" he yelled. She was nowhere in sight. He mounted the stairs, calling her name, making his way along the hall. Fire burned to either side. Soon the passage would be engulfed. No time to search. He must move on, take heed his dream. He cleared the final portal. There at the edge she stood looking downward, her face a mask of sorrow, eyes set on the body beneath. "Muriel, wait!" The familiar voice disrupted her dark reverie. She glanced round in doubt. "It's Henry! Come to me." He eased in her direction. Again, she stared at the prostrate form, her posture inclined as to welcome death. "No, darling! Don't!" She leaned. He lunged and caught her fall, pulling her close. Like a child, she submitted. Picking her up, he carried her down through the smoke and flames and out into the open air.

"Franz, the carriage! Get water! Have we a blanket and pillow?"

"In the trunk, sir."

"Good!" he said, placing her gently on the seat.

"Here you are."

"Right! Lead the horses away from the fire. I'll stay in the coach with her."

"Very well, sir." Calming the team with his hands, Franz coaxed them forward. The others had acted in like manner, not wishing their horses to bolt, and were waiting a fair ways off.

"Shall we leave him there?" Sven asked.

"What else can we do?" said Jan.

"Damn the villain!" Hans cursed. "Let him rot where he lies!"

"The wolves will get him if nothing else." As Jan spoke, the carriage pulled up. For a moment, all stared at the burning castle. "We'll lead!" Jan gestured, breaking the silence.

"Follow on!" Henry beckoned to Franz. A flash of lightning lit the sky. Thunder crashed overhead. The rain began, first slow, then steady and hard. They rode in silence, Muriel asleep in his arms.

The Curse

Dusk Entry

Dawn colored the eastern sky with reddish-yellow streaks. A teapot whistled and sputtered on Jan Schmidt's stove. The clockmaker took the kettle and filled two cups on the table.

"I appreciate your letting us stay over."

"Don't mention it, Heinrich. I trust the young lady is better today."

"I'm afraid for her, Jan. God knows what she's suffered, poor girl. What a frightful ordeal!"

"A bad business, that!"

"Let's hope there's an end!"

"Jan Kohlberg and the others will be here soon. If I know them, they'll have him buried straight and fast."

"I'd go with them, but I need to see Mother. And the carriage departs from the station at noon. If only we could stay a while longer."

"No, son. You're right about leaving. Take her from this place." He gazed out the window to the far horizon. "To visit the clock shops of Vienna!"

"You shall! You must come and stay with us soon!"

A cry made them stop and look upward. Henry, hurrying to the stairs and Muriel's room, found her in a nervous state of anxiety, shifting her head in confusion and pulling frantically at the covers.

"Muriel, look at me; it's Henry," he soothed, taking her hand. It was all he could do to calm her, caressing her forehead and hair. "You're safe with me, love." She closed her eyes, squeezing his hand, locked in a frame of repressed emotion. Her hand relaxed. He rose, kissing her brow, and left her to rest, closing the door.

"I'm bringing her with me to the convent. In her condition, there's no telling what might happen. I can't understand!"

"How's that?"

"Her behavior. Karloff had her in some sort of trance; so much I know. But to take his life, set fire to the castle! My Muriel?" Footsteps sounded on the stairs. "Franz, thank heaven it's you!"

"Sir?"

"Oh, what matter? Be a good fellow and have some tea, will you!"

"And breakfast," Jan offered.

"Hadn't I better see to the carriage, sir?" he replied, unsure of himself.

"Well, if you wish. But you must eat. Here, take some food along." As the butler retreated, a knock came at the door. In walked Jan Kohlberg, Sven Dyke, and Hans Beckner. Franz, plate in hand, escaped behind them out the door.

"He's an odd one by the make of him." Sven pointed with a thumb over his shoulder.

"Let be!" The shopkeeper waved, inviting them into the dining room.

"Damned if I could get those eyes from my sleep last night!" Hans stated.

"Not a pleasant sight," Sven agreed. "The sooner he's under ground the better, I say!"

"What sticks with me…" Jan began, then hesitated. "I ought to have mentioned it, but the fog. All the same, I'd swear he pushed her."

"Pushed her? What do you mean?" Henry asked.

"There on the roof, pushed her back as he fell. I can't say for certain, mind."

"Why do I have this nagging sense?" Hans shifted as though unsettled. "Confounded nerves, I suppose."

"Nerves or none, we've work to do."

"Will you stay for tea?" their host offered.

"No thanks! Sven's right; we'd best keep moving. And you, Heinrich?" As Jan spoke, standing by the table with the others, Muriel came from the stairs and stopped, frozen in place amidst the living room, looking like one who's lost her way.

"Muriel, dear!" Henry encouraged, going to take her hand. Weak and compliant, she went with him to the table as the men stepped aside. "We'll be leaving at noon," he told them.

"We understand. We'll see to everything," Sven promised.

"I'm much obliged!"

Muriel ate but little, sipping the tea, ill at ease with herself. When he felt she'd finished, Henry guided her upstairs and bid her prepare for the journey.

"I swear, Jan, she's like a wounded bird."

"She's a delicate creature, to be sure. But she'll recover, especially with your care."

"The trauma's too near, I suppose, too real in her mind. Travel's the very thing; the farther the better!" As he spoke, the clocks began to chime out of sync—seven o'clock!

Jan went to his counter. "I've kept this

to the last," he indicated, revealing the gold pocket watch.

"Why, it's good as new!"

"Almost! There's a part I must get in Vienna." He smiled.

"Splendid!"

"Of course, you may take it yourself."

"Nothing doing! It'll be waiting for you."

"Ah, such a timepiece is rare, indeed! I'm honored."

"The pleasure is mine. And now I'd best check on Muriel. We'll need to make haste." Ere long, they were out the door and into the carriage, Franz at the reins.

"Godspeed to you all!" Jan waved.

"See you before noon!" Henry promised.

They reached the convent grounds by nine and navigated the final turns bending up to the compound. Muriel, who'd slept the whole way, awoke with a start when the carriage halted. "We're here at Saint Ann's," Henry reassured, guiding her from the coach.

"Henry! Thank goodness you've come!"

"Mother, help me get her inside."

"This way; we'll take her for prayer."

Muriel moved in a fog, the voices muddled and faint. Once more she wandered the castle halls, her mind closed in on itself. "Henry?" She groped.

"I'm here, my love," he endeavored, holding her waist and hand. At length, they came to what looked like a chapel.

"Wait there,"—she indicated—"I won't be long."

A mourning dove cooed from a willow branch. Chimes rang in the breeze. He sat with her, feeling her helplessness.

Christina returned with Mother Germane and Sister Ann. "We must have time with her alone," the Reverend Mother stated after examining the girl. "You may show your son to the garden. Be back with us promptly."

"Yes, Mother."

"Does she know what she's doing?" Henry asked in their absence.

"It's God's work, son. We must believe and obey his will."

"But I've failed her, Mother."

"The failure is mine. Think no more of it. The garden is just beyond the greenhouse. Follow the path. Go!"

Afar to the north, three men rode up to the castle on horseback. "Let's dismount here and continue on foot," Jan suggested. Tying their horses to trees, they started across the front grounds.

"I say we move up easy," Hans cautioned. The others nodded, dreading the thought of that face. Ascending the slope, they wavered.

"Was it... was it not?"

"Preserve us!" Jan prayed, crossing himself.

Hans could but stare at the ground in horror.

"Sven, you take the left side; Hans, you the right. I'll head in from the center. Have your guns ready." Sweat formed on their brows as they moved in measured steps toward the castle. A raven croaked from the rooftop. The sun was warm on their necks.

"Over here!" Sven called. A knife shimmered off to the left. Reaching the spot, he pulled the blade from a post and showed it to the others.

"That's blood, all right," Jan remarked.

"Yes, but how did it get there?"

"We'd best have a look round the side."

Hans glanced about, not caring for the idea. "I say we leave. I've a bad feeling in my stomach."

"Hurry, Hans!" Sven motioned, following Jan's lead. But the grounds were barren and quiet.

"Look there!" Jan pointed toward the cliff, where a trail of smoke curled into the air. Leaving the castle, they pursued the path to the site of the ashes and smoldering cinders. Their faces dropped. Hans turned aside, his body doubled over. Sven grimaced. Jan wretched. Four wolf carcasses, burnt to the skin, were laid out around the fire pit, one slit open from neck to groin, heart and innards cut out.

"What devilry is this?" Sven's question was answered by Hans, who stumbled backward and was hastening up the path. He'd seen it first—the grave that appeared and loomed to their left in an ominous form.

"I'm with him. Let's move!"

"Right." Sven nodded, unable to fathom the scene. Hans was running, the others hard after, their fear being more of a surety that if they tarried they'd end as the wolves, an uncanny sense that carried them onward, straight to their horses and down the mountain. They didn't look back or feel at ease till they reached the moor beyond the forest.

In the garden, Henry noticed a nun bent over a bed of flowers, her head covered. He thought of Muriel and his mother's words: "The failure is mine. Go!" As he walked, he grew more in tune with his setting—the fragrant air, the color of leaf and flower, the shape...

"Theresa!"

She stood, trowel in hand. "Henry! Christina said you would come. It seems you've found me in my element. But I..."

"Thought I mightn't recognize you, I suppose. I'll admit you have changed."

"I'm still the same woman."

"Are you?"

"There's something I've wanted to tell you but somehow haven't been able. Our journey together..." she began. "Henry, I'm free!"

"Free?" he asked, uncertain.

"I'm going to Asia—to India. You see, I've decided to become a missionary."

"Good God! You can't be serious?"

"Perfectly! I've wanted to go ever since I was a little girl."

"I... don't know what to say."

"Be happy for me; that's all I ask."

"Happy? I guess if you'll be I can try. Only, isn't it? I mean..."

"Dangerous?"

He smiled. "I grant your point. Even so, India's more than a single river. Who'll be there to support you? You won't go alone surely."

"I will; that is, till I reach Mumbai."

"You've an escort?"

"To the mission station about forty miles inland."

"And these clothes?"

"I'll have a lighter outfit."

"Ah, there's some good in it, then."

"I did grow rather fond of feeling like a child again." She laughed.

"We were like children, weren't we?"

"Like Adam and Eve?"

"What a rapturous, playful creature you are! If only we could keep that time forever!"

"We might get rather hungry and tired, don't you think?"

"India,"—he shook his head—"well, that's that, then. May I write you at least?"

Their eyes met, hands joined. The time of temptation had come in all its heat of passion! Forbidden fruit, lips touching, a tear on her cheek.

"Good-bye, Henry. I'll always remember you."

"Good-bye," he sighed. "Take care of yourself!" Unable to bear the strain, he turned and parted.

Just then, Christina came round the greenhouse, Muriel at her side. "There you are, son!"

Muriel took in the scene—Henry leaving the nun, their faces, the glisten in her eye. "Henry!" She ran forward, throwing herself into his arms.

"What's this?" he marveled.

"Oh, darling, I've missed you!"

"Why, Muriel, you're recovered!"

"She'll need plenty of rest," Christina cautioned. "You must see that she eats well and has lots of liquids. Otherwise, I think she'll be fine."

"That's wonderful news! Just wonderful!"

"Is she a friend of yours, Henry?" Muriel asked, indicating Theresa.

For a moment, he hesitated. "An acquaintance," he said, hiding his true emotion.

"It's quarter to ten, Henry! You'd better be going if you're to catch the coach."

"I suppose you're right. Shall we, then?" So he left her there in the garden.

Vienna

Morning Entry

"Do you love me, dear?" Muriel asked from her bathroom at an inn where the coach had stopped for the night.

He was almost irritated by the question. All day long she'd probed him, pressed him on the subject. What could he do to show her, to get the memory of Theresa from his mind? Muriel was his fiancée, pledged to him for life. He'd almost lost her to the castle, the bondage of his family, Karloff! *Who am I to judge?* he thought and said again, "Darling, I've told you. What more can I say? What proof do you need of my love?"

She was in a state he could not understand, a condition she herself merely sensed. The nuns' prayers were strong, freeing her from the worst of the trauma. She'd felt the healing virtue of the sacred oil as the anointing flowed down and throughout her being. And yet a shadow remained, clung to her body. In desperation, she did what any woman in her position might do. No, it wasn't her nature or manner of upbringing. Nor could she predict his response. She acted in keeping with the most basic of human needs: self-preservation, the desire for belonging, acceptance, security. And more, their future and that of the child as well! "Stay with me tonight!"

He balked at her words. "But we aren't married. How can we?" She gazed at him abashed, her eyes filling with tears. *She's like a fragile shell*, he realized, saw anew. *She'll break if I falter—I who am to blame!* He reached out his hands. "Come to me," she heard him say. His arms enclosed her waist, eyes met hers, mouth kissed her forehead, cheek, lips. She gave herself, knew him, loved him, felt the strength of his seed. They were one.

> June 14, the year of our Lord, 1806. I write to you, Heinrich, six days after your departure from Steinburg. You must know, though it pains me, that Jan Kohlberg is dead. How can I tell it? He was found last night with a knife in his back, a knife belonging to Sven Dyke. The whole town is astir. Sven denies the charge, says he found the blade stuck in

a post at the castle. My mind is confused. I want to help him. But what can I do? They arrived that day in severe distress. Your coach had departed. I was busy with a patron and asked them to wait, yet, when I went out, no one! They'd failed to find Karloff's body; this much I discerned. When I saw Hans the next day, he spoke of the devil, of wolves cut apart and roasted alive. He was highly distraught, so I let the matter be. From Jan and Sven I could learn no more. Then the terrible news of Jan's murder. I went to Sven today in the prison. He was not himself. Terror has seized the town. Each night, wolves howl on the moor to the north. No one dares go anywhere near the area. Tomorrow I visit your mother at Saint Ann's, a day before Sven's trial on Friday.

Jan Schmidt

June 16, the year of our Lord, 1806. Dreadful events! Today at noon Sven Dyke was executed. It's hard to believe, the trial and hanging! Hans Beckner was to witness in Sven's defense. He's nowhere to be found. Some fear him dead. Few believed Sven's testimony, incredible as it was. Folks say he went mad. How can this be? I suspect some sort of foul play. Could Sven have been framed? I knew him well, even as I did Jan Kohlberg. Both were good men. Something got to their bones. But what, I ask myself? The wolves make matters worse. Never has there been such dreadful howling! The town is fraught with a kind of hysteria; it harbors ill. I am much vexed. Christina is my one consolation, and thinking of you there in Vienna. Perhaps I'll accept your invitation to visit; it may do me good. I'll speak with your mother of this next week.

Jan Schmidt

Dear Jan,
Arrived here in Vienna safely by coach yesterday, June 27. Have read your letters several times and find the news too much to comprehend. Jan Kohlberg murdered? Sven hanged? It's been barely a month! What could have happened? You must write and tell me more when you can. Muriel and I will soon be married. She wants the date moved up a month. I do hope you'll come and persuade my mother to join you. I ask as a

friend. With you she'll be safe and my mind at peace. Speak to her, Jan. Show her this letter. The wedding may not be delayed; I can't say why. There's room at my house for Franz as well. I'll hope to meet you all at the main station within the month. Mail goes by horse and rider, as you know, and will reach here before the coach. I am full of anticipation.

Heinrich von Lichtenstein

Dear Heinrich,
Received your post today, July 12, the year of our Lord. Am sorry to write that Hans is yet missing. There are more rumors about. Some say he, not Sven, is to blame for Jan Kohlberg's death, that he's fled in fear. Others speak of gypsies camped at the foot of the mountain where moor and forest meet, of movement up and down the main road leading to the castle. More than ever people fear the place, mistrusting the gypsy band whose coming coincided with the wolves' departure. Your mother has anticipated you, dear Heinrich. A week after my first letter, I went to see her as usual. Her mind was set on the trip to Vienna. She leaves tomorrow, but not

by public transport. Franz, who's been with me these weeks, you must know, will himself bring her in your family carriage. I must remain for the time being. For as to the castle, I am all uncertainty. How could Karloff be alive after such a fall? Might the gypsies have found the body and then killed Jan and taken Hans captive? I'll ride out in two days to meet these wanderers.

Jan Schmidt

Henry, alone in his study, put the letter down and walked to the window. *What madness*, he thought, *to go out there alone!* He paced the floor, reflecting over the letter, stopping once more at the eastern vista. "Damn it all, Jan, be careful!" he swore, angry with himself for having left.

Meanwhile, Muriel busied herself with wedding preparations. Her father was a doctor in Vienna, their family respected members of society. Invitations must be sent out, the celebration planned, her dress prepared—everything perfect! Her world had become a kind of menagerie—countless pieces of colored glass, each reflecting a part of her soul—competing emotions born of her frantic need to be loved and accepted. Her time of the month had come and gone. She was with child. Soon her father would know, would discern her condition. And yet she was safe, had given herself to Henry, but once; it was all she needed. The child was hers, would be theirs, might be theirs, in fact.

"Henry," she asked that Sunday as they strolled in the park, "if we had a child, would it please you?"

"A child! Good heavens, you can't mean?"

She nodded, eyes upturned in want of his support, approval, embrace. "Yes, dear, I'm afraid so."

"Afraid? You confound me! But how do you...? What difference! Darling, that's wonderful!"

"Is it?" she exclaimed. "Oh, I'm glad, relieved to hear you say so! You can't imagine how I've suffered."

Again her words struck him. Where was the innocent girl he'd known, had fallen in love with? Had it been real? "I'll walk you home," he said, taking her arm. Neither spoke. Each understood their separate roles. Their path was set. They were joined in meeting society's demands. In love? He glanced at her as they walked. She beamed, happy and radiant.

He took it for love, all he'd known, excepting Theresa. How would he feel were it she by his side?

His mother arrived with Franz a week later on a Sunday. The weather was wet and overcast, and he in his study was busy examining a family tree he'd found in a journal book—a parting gift from his mother—that had sat untouched on a shelf for years. The record, written on a large sheet of paper folded down to fit in a book, was opened and laid out on a desk. It began with Count Victor von Lichtenstein, grandfather to the notorious Karl von Lichtenstein, stressing the male line with capital letters. He'd just reached the name of his own father and was staring at a blank space where a sibling would be listed when he heard the carriage pull up without. Putting aside his question, he rose and went to meet them.

"Mother!" He waved as he left the front door. Franz had assisted her from the carriage and was busying himself with the luggage.

"Come; let's get you out of this rain. Franz, just set the luggage inside the main entry."

"As you wish, sir."

"Mother," he said when he felt she was settled, Franz in the kitchen preparing dinner, "I've something to show you." Taking her upstairs to the study, he pointed at the paper. She recognized it at once.

"I'd forgotten—the journal I gave you. It's been so long."

"Ten years to be exact. A wonder I never examined the gift! Why didn't you mention the family tree?"

"I thought you'd find it, I suppose."

"Naturally. Well, anyway, look here at this space—blank, you see. I mightn't have noticed but for the fact that it's the only line in the entire tree without a name."

"It has a name, Henry," she confessed, sitting down with a distant look. "You have an uncle."

He stared at her, dumbfounded. "Uncle," he repeated.

"I would have told you—wanted to tell you—but your father forbade me."

"Why, Mother?"

"Your uncle, Wilhelm Lichtenstein, a younger sibling like yourself, fell in love with a gypsy girl and ran off with her family. The girl was a great beauty; she captured Wilhelm's heart. When he returned years later, he was a changed man."

"Changed?"

"He'd been raised a Lichtenstein, forced by his father to master the black arts. He was, it seems, the equal in skill to your own father. But the gypsy girl, like me, believed in God."

"How do you know this?"

"I know because she is my sister."

"Your sister?" he marveled.

"Yes, Heinrich. She married Wilhelm, and I Victor. Yet she alone convinced her husband to share in her faith. Victor, the eldest, bound to his father, would not be moved."

"This is difficult to believe."

"You must believe, my son! When Wilhelm arrived, there was a terrible argument, a fight. Victor refused to listen, even threatened to kill his brother. What could Wilhelm do? He left, swearing never to return. Years went by. Karloff was born, then you. Then I received a letter from my sister, Maria. She and Wilhelm had settled in Vienna."

"Vienna? Good Lord!"

"It was all she wrote. Things grew worse at home. So I had you go. I thought with you in Vienna I could visit and hope—"

"To find them, of course! But Father prevented your coming; that much I suspected. Couldn't you have written?"

"He watched the mail, punished me,

blamed me for your absence. Not until his death was I able to write. By that time, years had passed with no word from Maria. My letter was returned—discovered by Karloff, who'd become like his father."

"And I, unable to write, could give you no aid," he regretted aloud.

"Henry, they could be here, somewhere in Vienna."

He thought for a moment. "The city register—might they be listed?"

"Somehow, I don't think so."

"You're right, I suppose. He'd wish to remain anonymous, and for good reason. All the same, I could check at City Hall. But wait! The Order of Divine Light; I know of the place! At least, I've been by that way."

"No, Heinrich, you mustn't!"

"How else, Mother? He could be a member. And if, as you say, he's a changed man, I'll find him so."

"Yet, what if otherwise?"

"I mightn't find him in any case. Still, I must try. The Order would likely meet on a Monday at noon, in keeping with the moon and sun."

"That's tomorrow."

"Yes!"

"Be careful, son!"

"I shall, I assure you. But now, let's speak no more of the subject. Get some rest. I'll call you for dinner."

The next day, while Christina and Muriel shopped, Henry made his way to the meeting hall of the private society. He might have been prevented his purpose but for his name. Indeed, he found the members so calculated to order, he'd barely a chance to inquire. It wasn't at all what he'd imagined—with capes and magic—rather, a gentlemen's club of wealthy professionals whose minds inclined toward the supernatural. None, he was told (as was assumed), had attained to Master of Divine Light status, such being considered a relic of the past. All believed energy to be the divine life—the quintessence in and from which the essences derived their nature and being. One believed in God in terms of Christian theology, yet secretly and alone, this being the founder himself, Wilhelm von Lichtenstein, who directed the gathering.

"I've awaited your coming, Heinrich," he said as the meeting ended and members departed. "Here, give me your hands." He did so, uneasy. "Look straight into my eyes! Ah, it's true! You have your mother's gift of life! She is here," he discerned. Henry waited, unable to speak. "There is trouble... fire in the castle! What's this?" He gazed in amazement. "Victor lives! What can it mean?"

"My father?"

"So this is the force behind your visit."

"I don't understand."

"Your father's shadow, even this moment, is over you. No, he's not dead. I see you wonder. His life force is strong. You too feel it but don't understand. Why do you think I remained a member of the Order, a secret master? I'll tell you. He sent his men, gave me no peace! What choice had I, with a wife and child? I attained to a level beyond his reach, established the Order here in Vienna, yet remained with my wife in mutual faith." He paused. "This thing in your heart, it cannot be done. You're no match for him, this image of Victor. He's far too powerful."

"He's alive?" Henry gaped.

"You thought him dead? No, Heinrich. Karloff lives and will be to you as Victor has been to me. You were wise to find me out. Wiser yet is your mother. Her prayers have protected you."

"What then should I do?"

"We must face him!"

"We?"

"Hush! Listen! I hear a child, see a woman."

"Muriel!"

"You must tell me everything!"

"My fiancée, she's been with child these past two months."

"What day? Pray, be exact!"

"Let me think. June … 6! Yes, I'm ashamed to admit."

"Something is wrong, very wrong. I must speak to her."

"Tomorrow say, can you come for dinner?"

"To be sure! Maria will see her sister. And I shall meet your Muriel; she it is who holds the answer."

Henry left the hall in a sweat, his pulse racing and mind a blur. Never had he met such a man as his uncle. He trembled, calmed himself, and hailed a carriage.

Wilhelm and Maria arrived at precisely six o'clock the next evening in a lovely carriage of polished black with velvet red cushion seats.

"Maria! Is it possible?" Christina exclaimed, embracing her sister with tears of joy.

The dinner was pleasant, with roast lamb prepared and served by Franz. Wilhelm gave no sign of his mastery. He listened politely and added his part to the conversation. This too impressed Henry and heightened his esteem of the man. *A considerate, even humble Christian gentleman, yet a Master of Divine Light*, he puzzled. *How can this be?*

They finished dessert. Christina and Maria excused themselves and went to the parlor to visit in private. Suddenly, as if planned, they were alone—he, Muriel, and his uncle.

"Heinrich tells me your father is a doctor—a fine physician!"

"I thank you, sir! He's very dear to me."

"He helped me establish my own practice," Henry noted with gratitude.

"Well, you'll be in good hands when the child is born."

Muriel glanced at Henry uneasily.

"No, my dear, Heinrich revealed nothing of this matter, as he himself will confirm."

She saw it was so. "Then you... are a soothsayer."

He laughed. "If you wish. Will you lend me your hand?"

She hesitated, but only for a moment. "What harm can there be?"

"Good!" the distinguished guest encouraged. She was in his sway yet felt at peace, her nature to yield satisfied.

"You hold a deep secret," he began, his

right hand on her head and left supporting her upturned palm. "Close your eyes. What do you see?"

"A road, a castle, I … "

"Go on."

As he spoke, she began to rock backward and forward. "It's dark, so very dark."

"Where are you? Tell me."

"I can't say." She strained.

"Forgive me; I must take you deeper," he said, placing both hands on her head and shutting his eyes.

"Henry!" she called out.

"I see him, this man. He has you in bonds! What's this? You think him Heinrich?" She swayed as he spoke. Henry moved but was eased by Wilhelm's hand. "You are dancing, laughing. You stop, hear a carriage."

"Oh, Henry, you've come!"

"Look close! Is it he?"

"No,"—she waved her head—"no, you're not Henry."

"He's left! You are in a tunnel, a hallway of some sort, fighting to stay awake."

"I must! I must!" She breathed heavily, groping with her hands.

"You need air! You must have air!" He was breathing with her.

"Air!" she gasped.

"The window, you've opened it. You see him!" Suddenly, she stood, head reeling in her hands with confusion. Again, the signal, stopping Henry. "You know!" he compelled. "You must say it!"

"I hate him! Hate him!" she fumed, hands clenched, head moving as if in search of a weapon.

"Where have you gone?"

"I've found him!" She bristled, her face wrought with fury. "Villain! Villain!" she cried, stabbing at the air.

"Why? Tell me why."

"He deceived me, violated me!" She sobbed, slowing her movement, collapsing in a convulsion of tears.

He caught her, gave her into Henry's arms. The women arrived. "Take her upstairs," Wilhelm bid. "Let her rest. That's good. She'll be fine now." They enfolded her and led her apart in sympathy.

"My God—the castle! Jan said Karloff pushed her back, prevented her fall! How could I have failed to see the truth?"

"You believed what you wished to be so; it is common enough."

"Better I learned—was made to face reality. But, Uncle, we don't know that the child is Karloff's. Do we?"

"In any case, she'll need your support. More than this I can't say at present."

"I understand. Thank you for your aid. What a burden it must have been, carrying that awful secret!"

While the sisters comforted Muriel, the two men visited, Henry getting to know his uncle—this elder—so different from his father and yet his father's brother.

"The evening's been most insightful," Wilhelm announced, hearing the women's step on the stairs. Henry took his hand gratefully.

"Thank you for coming!"

"My pleasure, Heinrich! Until next time."

"Yes."

"Maria, the carriage!"

Riding the Storm

Noon Entry

July 14, the year of our Lord, 1806. Strange news. I've been to the gypsy camp these past two days. The first day I was met with much suspicion. They were uncooperative and gave me no answers. The road to the castle was blocked, I noticed. When I asked why, they grew uneasy, denying my wish to go up the mountain. What can this mean, I asked myself. There was no threat of violence, yet it was clear they desired my absence. What was I to do? I left, resolving to return the next day with watches and other items to trade in hope of winning their trust. They made light of my goods. Apparently someone had paid them much more. I rode to the south toward town then circled back, approaching from the east along the mountain's base. From deep in the trees I watched as they hauled loads of planks and other building materials. How can I describe what happened next? It was more a presence, a feeling of danger. My horse stirred uneasily. I searched the woods; no one. And then I saw it—a cloaked form with eyes that burned like fire. I tried to run, but my feet wouldn't move. Those hideous eyes! I looked aside then back. No one! I fled, my heart racing, down and out through the trees, onto my horse and across the moor. My hand yet trembles as I write these words. Was it real, this phantom? Might I be overwrought from too much stress? Could it have been Karloff? I must rest. Tomorrow I leave by coach and hope to be in Vienna on schedule.

Jan Schmidt

It was Wednesday morning, July 29. Muriel had left with Wilhelm and Maria the previous night, accepting their offer of a ride home, much to Henry's surprise. A shadow had passed from her life; this much he detected. But whose was the child? Only time would tell. And yet he was pained, cut by the thought that it could be his brother's. He'd be at the meeting next Monday, as asked. Maybe Wilhelm meant to give him some counsel.

The day went by without event, then a second day. Toward evening, the sky darkened. The air grew calm. A storm was brewing. It broke in fury of lightning and thunder, exciting the atmosphere with streaks of electric current that flashed overhead, giving way to a torrential downpour falling in sheets that reflected the light above yet changed to floods of water pouring from roofs and windows, turning the lanes and walks of Vienna into a living stream. Friday arrived in wary alertness, people relieved to feel the sun and find the city as ever it was. Jan too was pleased to reach the outskirts and make his way over shiny streets to the home of his friends.

"Jan Schmidt!" Henry exclaimed, overjoyed to see the clockmaker's face.

"You received my letters," Jan gathered, taking Henry's hand.

"Yes, I did. We'll have plenty of time to talk. Let me carry some of your things."

"And Christina?"

"She's fine, Jan; eager to see you!"

Dinner that night was alive with news of Steinburg, the gypsies, and the tragic events that led to his journey. "It's a different town," Jan concluded. "I'd never have believed! People I've served—known for a lifetime—filled with mistrust and suspicion, just like the gypsy band."

"These gypsies, can you describe them?" Henry asked. "My father, some years before I left, used to hire such labor."

"They're about fifty in number, a large group. Typical, I suppose: colorful clothing, jewelry, head covers. Peaceful enough, I'd say, though rugged. Peculiar folk."

"In any case, they've no business there. And Karloff, if he lives—"

"Must be left alone!" Christina stressed, relieved she'd kept her past to herself.

"What do you think, Jan?"

He fretted, perturbed, recalling the dire vision. "I'm here," he replied. "I imagine that says it all."

"We're glad! Tomorrow the city waits. There's an impressive clock shop just down the way, in fact."

"That's better!" Christina approved. "I'll go with you!"

By ten the next morning the two had gone off, leaving Henry behind in his study. Franz came to the door. "A visitor, sir." He stepped aside, and there stood Wilhelm.

"Thank you, Franz! Uncle Wilhelm, what a surprise!"

"Close the window!" He motioned, his eyes searching the room. "You have something to give me—news of some sort."

Henry did as requested, reflecting. "The letters!"

"Where are they? Show me!"

Taking Jan's letters from the desk, he gave them to his uncle, who stood transfixed, as one bent on discerning the cause of some new concern.

"This Jan Schmidt, he is come, no?"

"Just yesterday!"

"Ah,"—he nodded—"as I thought." Henry waited, tense with anticipation yet alive with sudden awareness. "Karloff, your brother, has found you out, followed Jan to your house."

"Great thunder!"

"He's cunning, this Karloff. Jan, I've no doubt, is ignorant of the matter, driven more by fear than need. Think, Heinrich! Would Karloff have let him go without cause? I say this for your own sake, for I saw him coming the night of the storm."

"But why, Uncle?"

"At first I thought it the girl he wanted. You he would kill, only if necessary. Yet his pride exceeds even that of my brother. He will be as the storm—forceful, violent! And we shall be ready!"

"How?"

"Listen to me. Do exactly as I say. Remain in this house. Send nothing and no one to Muriel. I myself will bring word that you're to be my guest for three days. Be ready to leave with Christina at seven tonight. Do not venture out till you see my face or look from the carriage windows. Understand?"

"Yes, Uncle!"

"Good! I bid you farewell!"

"Are you sure he said three days, Heinrich? What about Jan and Franz?" Christina asked later.

"We'll get on," Jan assured. "I've more shops to visit. And Franz and I are used to each other."

"It's good of you, Jan!"

"Well, I'd best get ready," she resigned.

At seven o'clock sharp, the coach pulled up to the front. Christina bid Jan good-bye as Franz assisted with bags and Henry her ascent to the seat. *Odd,* she thought, *that Wilhelm waits at the reins.* Franz closed the door. They were off at a steady pace, the window shades closed.

By Sunday evening, Henry'd almost forgotten the warning of danger. Never had he been so contented, except at times with Theresa.

From the moment they pulled in the drive to the present hour, he'd experienced a realm of complete harmony. Rooms were arranged for this or that purpose: art, music, science, reading, carpentry, drafting, cartography, and more. What days they'd spent as the sisters talked and did as they pleased.

"You've learned well, Heinrich! And we've freed ourselves of care for a time. It is fitting, for tomorrow will try our resolve, to be sure."

"He'll be there?"

"I have no doubt."

"What then?"

"We'll get to the center at eleven o'clock, as is my custom. He'll come at noon, but only to force you away."

"And you?"

"He suspects. Victor has made him wary. I will hide my strength, however, in hope of persuading him."

"What of the others?"

"They'll watch and discern. They are gentlemen, all, in terms of conduct, noble in deed. Many, however, think the Order a way to God; in this they're mistaken, and I'm to blame in part. What roles we play in our private need," he reflected. "Yet the time may come—and soon—when I shall close the doors for good. But now it's late, and we must rest."

Monday arrived in a heat of anticipation. Wilhelm, Heinrich noticed, evinced no sign of unease. Morning wore on. They left for the hall. Members showed up. The hour reached twelve—the zenith of fire! Henry looked down from the upper balcony area to the circular floor beneath. A round table, divided into four sections with one missing to the south, defined the space. The members, who usually sat at the table, surrounded the balcony and with him waited in expectation. All eyes were fixed on Wilhelm, who stood below to the south in silence. Above, a precise depiction of the starry heavens covered the grand domed ceiling; to its center, a window of glass looked up to the sky. Suddenly, the men shifted and gazed at a stranger who entered and caused them to look at Heinrich and then back in bewilderment.

"At last you are here—the image of Victor. What news do you bring me?"

Circling the room from east to north, Karloff stared in defiant response. "Why do you meddle in my affairs, Uncle? You, who my father despised! You were wise to leave."

"And you foolish to stay."

"You presume to test me?"

"Rather, I remind you, you stand in a temple of peace. And I, the master here, request you obey the Order."

The two men faced each other across the floor. Above, each member felt a strain, a pressure as of two forces colliding yet held in tension.

"An empty command from a false teacher, a gypsy vagrant too jaded to ever be a real master! I would teach you and all this idle band!"

Some rose but soon reseated themselves in honor of Wilhelm's request. "Have you nothing better to offer, Karloff? No honor, respect for an uncle and elder?"

"I want only Heinrich. With you I've no quarrel. Though well would my father commend me for striking."

"To hurt or kill as the others have tried? Be prudent and learn from their failure."

"What wisdom have you? What ability? I see merely a man who would play with words."

"Then I will speak plainly. Heinrich is an honored guest of this assembly. He is my charge; the child, my charge."

"The child is mine; I shall have it! Or have you forgotten the ways of old?"

"Ways of our fathers, corrupted by pride and deceit? This is your motive?"

"I'll crush you in a moment! On what authority do you speak? Answer me!"

"Take heed, I warn you, as you are my blood, the son of my brother. His spirit is heavy upon you, Karloff. I give you a choice. Surrender your aim and have my pardon. Repent of this evil I see in your heart!"

"You persist?"

"I implore you!"

"Implore? A woman's words! Be done!" He lighted atop a table, looked at Heinrich, and then landed amid the enclosure, facing Wilhelm.

"Gentlemen, today our guest will demonstrate his skills in the martial arts. Remember," he stressed, "I've encouraged you to avoid such use of power."

Stung by the words, Karloff circled the inner floor in step with his uncle, their minds locked in a private battle. He'd underestimated his strength. Fire met water, sword metal of finer make and action. Daggers were directed aside with a flash of the eyes. Blow after blow was deflected. Wilhelm stood, calm, immovable, the consummate master.

"Magic will not serve you!" he cautioned.

Scorning the threat, he flew upward in Heinrich's direction but soon was met in the air and forced down, his flurry of hits repulsed.

Again the men stood face to face. They seemed to converse without a word. For a time, Karloff waited, unwilling to yield. Then, all of a sudden, he bowed and departed swift as he'd come.

"Gentlemen, the demonstration has ended. I would ask you to retire and do as you please. William, will you lead the meeting next week?"

Astonished along with the others, he nodded consent.

"Thank you! Good day to you all!"

"What will he do?" Heinrich asked when the members had left.

"Come; we must go to your house at once! The letters! There's something I've missed. Hurry!"

Hastening down, Heinrich went with his uncle to the carriage and thence with speed to his house and study.

"Where are they?"

"Here!"

Taking the letters, he paced the room, reading them over and over then laying them on the desk. "What a fool I've been! So focused was I on Karloff, I failed to see the full meaning of Jan's report."

"I don't follow."

"Sit down, Heinrich. Take up the notes. Is there anything unusual, do you think? Look close."

"Now that you mention it, I'm inclined to agree with Jan about the murder."

"Why?"

"As he says, these were honorable men."

"Precisely! And so?"

"You mean to say Jan was right, that Sven was framed? But who would do such a thing? What could be the motive?"

"That, it seems, we must find out. What else?"

"The band of gypsies! And the roadblock!"

"Then too the knife, the sacrificial offering of wolves and use of vital organs for healing, the luring of the pack to the moor. Do you see the pattern?"

"Of course; he was injured! He was protecting himself from something."

"Or someone. And I, being ignorant of the matter, failed to warn the men who perished."

"Warn?"

"Yes, Heinrich. You see, they were in my service, or had been so in the past."

"Good Lord!"

"I knew them well. And when your father was killed, I had them keep watch on Karloff for a time."

"Because you suspected him?"

"Until today when I read his mind. He is but a reflection, as I deduced." Going to the window, he searched the sky then paced the room in agitation. "Confound it!" he swore. "There must be a clue! Heinrich, give me your hand. Maybe you've seen or heard the answer without realizing."

"Here," he offered.

"Close your eyes. I want you to reflect. Focus your mind on unsolved matters, however trivial, anything that you found unusual. There, good, I see you with Muriel. You want to enter a place of sanctuary but cannot. Why? Do you remember?"

"Saint Ann's! The nun at the gate."

"What did she say?"

"To return in the morning. I can't recall why."

"Try, Heinrich!"

"The wolves! It's all just a blank."

"I remove the block from your mind," Wilhelm uttered. "In the name of Jesus, you are freed from this curse!"

Henry shook in response. "I see her now!"

"She speaks! Tell me!"

"She says there's no one by that name in the convent."

"Of Lichtenstein?"

"Yes!"

"What else?"

"That she has her orders."

"There!" he concluded, releasing his hands. "We have the key!"

"But how?"

"Next Monday after the wedding we leave for Saint Ann's. I'll explain on the way."

"What of Muriel and Mother?"

"Don't worry. They'll be good company. And your mother can visit with Maria."

"I see. Well then, Franz will be here to look after their needs, I suppose."

"As for Karloff, you may be at peace. I impressed on his mind that the child is yours. He won't remain."

"Is it, Uncle?"

"Only God knows. Let us look to him, for our greatest trial is yet ahead."

Avenging Root

Evening Entry

Wilhelm and Heinrich reached Saint Ann's on a Friday, nineteen days after the wedding. The journey from Vienna had allowed them time to become well acquainted, and a bond had formed like unto that of father and son. Muriel, Henry knew, was safe and well. Even Jan Schmidt, delighted with the city and being asked to work at a local shop, had decided to stay, at least until Heinrich returned.

The August air was hot and sultry as they approached what to Heinrich was the familiar nun's convent. "We've come to speak with Sister Germane," he informed the novitiate who met them at the front and after having them wait escorted them with some reluctance to the waiting Mother Superior.

"To say I'm surprised by your visit would be an understatement," she admitted, welcoming the men. "What business could bring you all this way after so brief an interval? It must be urgent, indeed!"

"The matter is, in fact, of such a nature that only a note from my mother will suffice to explain. We ourselves are but searching for answers. Please, if you'd be so kind as to read this," Heinrich asked, handing her the letter.

"You read it,"—she gestured with a nod—"as the subject concerns you, I expect. Best I hear it from your own lips."

"If you prefer," he submitted.

"Please, do be seated, gentlemen."

> Dear Reverend Mother, I write you from Vienna, where circumstances prevent my presence. Surely Heinrich will explain. What he's failed to reveal, however, I must here convey. It concerns the day he and Muriel first came to Saint Ann's wishing to see me; this would have been the second day of June, in the afternoon. Sister Caroline, on duty at the gate, refused them entry on the order of Sister Margaret; yet, though I was in sanctuary, everyone knew my concern excluded my youngest son. I write not to judge my sisters but to reveal the indirect consequences of their actions. That same evening Heinrich and Muriel were

denied respite and lodging in Steinburg, people suspicious and Jan Schmidt being out with relatives. Thus they were forced to go on by night to the castle. There in the forest they were attacked by wolves. Heinrich was badly injured. The rest you know—my trip with Theresa the next day and all that followed. Though, I'd add, had my son and daughter-in-law been allowed to stay at the convent the day before, Theresa would never have been held captive, nor would Muriel. Why Sister Margaret and Sister Caroline acted as they did I don't know. Only it seems some confession is needed. That is all. I covet your prayers and remain faithful to Christ.

Sister Christina

Taking a bell in hand, the Mother Superior rang for assistance. "Sister Ann, have Sister Caroline brought here at once."

"Yes, Reverend Mother."

"I'm sorry to report, gentlemen," she said, standing, "that Sister Margaret is absent."

"Absent? How do you mean?" Heinrich asked.

"It appears she simply left without a word."

"What day, pray?" Wilhelm pursued.

"Just yesterday. She's been with us these past twenty-one years. And though she came to us in great distress, she's been faithful to the Order of Saint Benedict. We're much concerned and doing all that we can to find her."

"Did she ever show signs of strain after her arrival?"

Wilhelm's question made her hesitate. "A few years ago, when the late Victor von Lichtenstein was killed, she was...let's say, she was not herself. I thought it odd, but as the condition passed I forgot. Then, when Sister Christina came, she seemed to struggle. Oh, it wasn't Christina's fault; rather, if you'll pardon my saying, her family background that made Sister Margaret suspicious, even envious." As she said this, the bell rang and Sister Ann appeared with Sister Caroline, who looked about uneasily.

"Come, my daughter; you've nothing to fear." Mother Germane signaled. "Sit here beside me." The others sat. "Now, tell me what you can about Sister Margaret. We've had a letter, you see, that indicates she asked you to prevent this gentleman's entry into Saint Ann's. You aren't to blame, child. But you need be open and forthright. Sister Margaret is missing. And we must consider everything in hope of finding her."

Tears were forming in the novitiate's eyes. "Forgive me, Mother."

"Yes, yes, I forgive you."

Wilhelm, meanwhile, unnoticed by all but the novitiate, had caught her eye. He perceived by her behavior that she wouldn't confess without aid. In fact, she held the key he needed. He must draw her out! To the astonishment of everyone, the girl became composed and sat upright.

"I'll tell you everything I know," she said. In her mind, her hands were in his. She was in his hold—caught up in a vision—yet looked at the Mother Superior as she spoke. So began the account the girl had heard from Margaret's own lips of the terrible rape, the period of waiting, her fleeing for refuge to the convent and care of the nuns.

And more, she spoke of Bruno Kraus, the man who took the infant child—how he came to hear of Heinrich's return, the fire at the castle, the report of three men who'd ridden up the next day. He went himself to speak with Jan Kohlberg, plying him for answers. Why had they gone? What did they find? Jan, heedless of danger, confessed to his aiding of

Heinrich. Seeing the buck knife handy, Bruno bided his time and struck! It was evening and small effort to place the knife at the shop of Sven Dyke, whom he later accused of murder. Now he'd focus on Karloff, who he knew was wounded. Again, his efforts failed.

He must find a means, another way! Then it occurred to him: what if the gypsies were the same band? If so, he could seek the nun who'd mothered the child and use her to his own ends. How? Simple! Convince her of his innocence. Say he'd taken the child out of sympathy, raised him like a son. Make it seem an act of atonement if need be. Only get her and Earl to stir up the gypsies against their oppressors, the Lichtensteins. Little could he know how well it would work. He went to the gypsy camp to be certain then waited his chance. After all, they were fixing the castle at Karloff's expense. Let them labor. In due course, he would contact Margaret, take her in private to meet her son, let her stay the night. The rest would be easy.

Caroline felt the hands withdraw. She looked at Wilhelm as though expecting his praise.

"I am sure she speaks the truth," he commended, breaking the lapse of silence.

"Mercy, child! How did you learn these things? Such a story!"

"From Sister Margaret, Mother. But I promised to keep it a secret. What will she think?"

"She'll thank you, no doubt!" Looking at her guests, she added, "We must find her soon."

"This Bruno Kraus, do you know where he lives?" Wilhelm asked.

"We went to his farm before giving over the child. Sister Margaret knew nothing of this I'm certain. We wanted to protect her. It all seemed proper at the time."

"I understand."

"I'll make you a map."

"Good. Thank you!"

"Sister Ann, take Sister Caroline to the prayer chapel. I'll be with you shortly."

"Yes, Reverend Mother."

"I've lived too long, gentlemen," she sighed. "I know this land like the back of my hand. To think, such dreadful doings! I shall try to forget. Ours is a peaceful life here at Saint Ann's. Sister Margaret is part of our family. Be assured we'll hold you in prayer."

"We'll do our best to bring her back safely," Wilhelm vowed.

"There you are," she said, handing the map to Heinrich, the action breaking his absent reflection.

"Thank you!" he managed.

"We've no time to lose!" Wilhelm prompted.

"Good-bye! God be with you both!"

"Good-bye!" they replied.

"Is it possible?" Heinrich asked as they made their way to the house of Bruno Kraus.

"Hmmm...yes, she has many gifts, that girl, including clairvoyance. With my help she took the strands of Margaret's story and that of the note she surely read and made her oration. Marvelous!"

"And the part about Jan and Sven? You don't mean!"

"She'd news of the trial. She had, in fact, all the evidence the mind of a seer would need to put the whole thing together."

"Marvelous, indeed!"

"But now we must focus on what's before us. Margaret is ignorant of Bruno's real motives. She thinks him an advocate."

"How? He was instrumental in her rape."

"Do you suppose a man as clever as he would be so careless? No, I assure you. He used another means, perhaps a servant, to render the keys into Margaret's hand and bid her do as the owner directed."

"And she, convinced she served as a maid, went to her fate like a thing of prey. I loathe the evil of my family! It is why I left. Will I ever be free?"

"You forget! I too left the castle. And I imagine your mother did so the day of the feast."

"She did. She took us to stay with Jan Schmidt. Even then he was a good friend."

"And she a good mother. No wonder you came out so well."

"You're right. I owe her much."

"And we've much to set right, you and I."

At length, they came to the mark on the map. "Here we are. This must be the place."

"Looks empty. What do you think?"

Wilhelm seemed to not hear. He was on the ground checking tracks, blades of grass, framing the action in time and place. "They left at noon—an hour, two at the most I'd say. Hurry; we must move on. To the camp of the gypsies!"

As they rode, a circle of clouds closed in overhead. A summer storm was in the making, the moorland showing the colors and shades of a changing sky. At half past three they reached the camp. Two men, rifles in hand, kept watch over the women and children.

"What might you be after?" one asked, his gun ready.

Heinrich would have replied in anger, but Wilhelm prevented him. "We've come in peace. We're looking for the owner of the castle on the hill."

The gypsy lowered his gun. "Huh! He'll be hung up high by now, I expect."

"Hung!" Heinrich started.

"They took a rope and plenty of guns. Appears as if you're too late!" He laughed. "By the way, what is your business?"

"That's our affair. What business have they to seek his life?"

"Who are you to ask?"

"Wilhelm Lichtenstein. Now how about an answer?"

"I'll give you this." He glared, raising his gun. The gypsy yelled and let loose the weapon, shaking his burnt hands.

"I'm sorry. You ought to have listened," said Wilhelm. The other man aimed and suffered the same fate. "Heinrich, the rifles."

"You may get by us, but you won't them!" the one declared.

"That too is our concern," he countered. "But tell me this: of what is he charged?"

"Murder, that's what! His father, curse him, raped one of our women. We thought her dead. But no! She comes to us this very day; a nun she is, with two men besides. They laid it out plain. We've no reason to doubt."

"Where is she?"

"You won't find her here. She's gone to the convent with one of our men."

"Is that all?"

"All you'll get from me!" He scowled.

"Then we'll be off. You'd best stay put!"

"Harsh words from a man who's about to die!"

"Empty the guns, Heinrich, then give them back. Do it! They've kin to look after."

"Hang the lot of you!" the leader yelled as they sped from the camp toward the mountain.

"Why didn't we see her on the road?"

"They saw us first, I suspect, and went from the way," Wilhelm answered. "This Bruno Kraus is a real devil. He even anticipates our coming, or rather hopes we do."

"Devil, indeed!"

"He'll find us fitted, you may be sure!"

"And the charge of murder?"

"A smokescreen of sorts."

"Jan Kohlberg you mean?"

"Yes."

"Why, the villain!"

"Take care! Follow my lead. Remember, I've told you, never be led by emotion!"

"Right!"

Ere long, they were high up the mountain and nearing the site of the wolf attack. Leaving the carriage, they continued on foot to the final bend in the road. There, at a stone's throw, stood a gypsy guard. In moments the gun was dropped and the man froze in a sort of daze. "Come," Wilhelm beckoned, emptying the rifle.

"Look, the place is surrounded!"

"There's one man I seek, one alone. Stay low! Say nothing for your life!"

"We know you're in there!" they heard a man shout. "Come out with your hands held high!"

"Over here!" another directed. "He's up on the tower!" So focused were they on their aim, they failed to notice the two who approached but instead moved in haste toward the cry and ground surrounding the tall structure.

"Shoot for the chest, men!" a tall gypsy ordered.

"They must be twenty in number," Heinrich observed.

"And each with a rifle. Bruno's doing, no doubt. Keep down. Wait! I want to be certain."

A volley of shots rang out.

"I got him!" one boasted.

"I must have hit him!" another avowed.

Just then, Wilhelm saw the man he wanted. By his side stood a younger man, mute and servile.

"I'll have his head! Do you hear?" Bruno shook his fist.

"Then you'd have mine too!"

The men turned, en masse, and stared at the two who came out of nowhere.

"Who the deuce are you?" the leader, a man by the name of Eric Hildebrand, demanded.

Bruno, however, stood forward and taunted, "Why, Wilhelm and Heinrich, you're just in time to meet the new master. May I present to you Earl von Lichtenstein." The latter looked up from the ground, unsure of himself. "You thought to rescue Karloff, I suppose."

"He's falsely accused!" said Wilhelm.

"He has murdered!" the gypsy declared. "He'll pay, as will you if you meddle!"

"What evidence did you give these men, Bruno Kraus? What proof of this charge?"

"We've proof enough," said Eric. "The word of my sister, whom his father raped! And who might you be?"

"They, my friend, are Karloff's uncle and brother given into your hand."

"Uncle and brother? Damn you all! Had I known what I learned today, I'd have done this years ago!"

"Please, don't act in haste," said Wilhelm. "I deeply regret the sin of my brother, the harm he did."

"Regret! What good are your words?"

"Kill them all, I say!" Bruno incited.

Wilhelm's arm held Heinrich back.

"Take three men," Eric answered. "Do as you will, only not here. Go yonder to the cliff. We'll stay and be sure of the other." Little did he realize as he spoke that Wilhelm himself had suggested the thought to his mind.

"Get on with you!" said Bruno.

"Trust me," Wilhelm whispered as they walked down the path toward the canyon and fire pit.

"Stop! This will do. Come, Wilhelm; I want to see you beg before you die."

"Tell me, Bruno Kraus, what made you betray my brother, a friend of yours?"

"Friend? Surely you jest!"

"As you jested the night you encouraged his lust?"

"How would you know?"

"You planned it all out, didn't you—even forged a will, no doubt."

"You're wrong! He wrote the will himself."

"Leaving everything to Earl, might I guess. What, in a drunken state? Your knife ready! Was it then you struck?"

Heinrich watched with concern as Bruno raised his rifle to shoot then dropped the weapon, swearing.

"You'd be wise to retreat," Wilhelm told the others, who instead felt the same effect of flashing eyes and burning metal. They gaped in awe while holding their hands. "Now the truth comes forth! It was you, Bruno Kraus, who murdered my brother! You who killed Jan Kohlberg, your blade in his back! Confess! Repent of your evil!"

"I'll do better!" he snarled, pulling a long knife from his belt. As he did, the others moved away, not for the act but the grave that appeared. They rubbed their eyes. There it stood and more—a whole graveyard! Turning aside, they fled in fear.

"What's happening?" Heinrich panicked.

"The curse of our family!" Wilhelm warned, edging off in distress.

Bruno too, seeing the graves round about, dropped his weapon and stood in horror. For there, close before his face, a tombstone arose. He tried to move, to run, but found his feet held tight by curling roots. "Save me!" he pleaded. Wilhelm caught Heinrich. The gypsies looked back. On the tombstone gleamed the name Karl von Lichtenstein!

The earth gave way. The roots, like clawing fingers, ripped and pulled at their victim's flesh. "No!" he screamed, thrashing about, flailing the roots in a futile attempt. The claws held firm, intent on their foe—the snapping of bones and press of blood. Down he went—legs, waist, chest, head, hands drawn under into the fissure, never to return. The graveyard vanished! The men caught their breath.

"God save us all!" Heinrich exclaimed.

"Up, let us go! I've no knowledge of this!" As they ran, they saw the fire ahead.

"They're burning him out!"

"Stay with me," Wilhelm guided.

The fire moved swiftly. The entrance, halls,

windows—all were alight! "There he is!" someone gloated. High on the tower, he stood and faced the men below.

"We've got him now!" a second hooted, raising his gun with the others. Another volley of shots went off. The men gawked, for before their eyes, the figure dissolved in a cloud of smoke. Then in reaction, a series of flaming arrows emerged, aimed at the four who'd started the fire. Dropping their torches, they cried in pain.

"Get back, everyone!" Eric commanded. In answer, a long and threatening howl went out from the tower, echoed by others away in the forest. "Run for your lives!"

"No!" Wilhelm warned. "To run is death! Stay close as you can to the main castle. They won't come near for fear of the flames. Take the torches and carry these men."

Eric hesitated, regarding the man he'd just condemned.

"Hurry, why don't you?"

"You heard him!" He signaled.

"Heinrich, take Earl and keep him close."

"Let me stay and fight!"

"Just do as I ask."

He conceded reluctantly, guiding his charge apart with the others.

"What next, Uncle?" Karloff mocked. "Will you test the wolves as you did me? Will they be your sport?"

"Better die than fear!"

"Well said! I applaud! But you who withstood me before a crowd—a rabble of fools—you shall do both!"

Unmoved by the words, Wilhelm held his ground. Lightning flashed across the sky. The wolves came out of the western trees, wary at first of the flames and men then eager in spying the figure alone.

"Here you are, Uncle, a host to serve you! Now let us see of what you are made!"

Following the lead, the pack closed in, all eyes set on the open prey. Ready, fearless, facing the tower, Wilhelm appealed in a final attempt: "Stand with me! Be free of your pride! Let go this curse that has plagued our family!"

"You, a rebel, command me yet? I'll slay you myself!" Drawing his sword, his cape spread out in posture of flight, he jumped to the ledge!

The lead wolf leaped. A blinding streak and shock of current struck the heights! The wolves laid down, the lead meeting air then heat of rage as Wilhelm moved and ignited in flame the presumptuous beast. But the pack looked elsewhere—there to the figure amidst the fire—the thunderbolt by which he fell! His sword let loose and, blazing downward, stuck in the ground by the great wolf's head! Staring in awe at the man before them, they stood up warily and turned about. They'd seen enough! Tails held low and heads set apart, they scampered away in a flurry of whimpers, fleeing into the eastern woods.

Epilogue

Twilight Entry

In the town of Steinburg far in the hinterland lives an old man. And if he could speak, he'd tell of a woman—a nun who left for Asia to serve the poor. Yet of a girl, young and fair, filled with fancy and secret desires, he'd only sigh and search the wooden boards of his floor. Her grave was set in a peaceful slope by a church in the city of Vienna. A smaller grave too was set by her side—that of a child born out of time. He might have lived in the castle Lichtenstein, this son, had fate not ended his life and that of his mother's at birth.

Reaching a weathered hand into his frayed jacket, he takes out a pocket watch worn with age. On its gold lid, engraved in fine lettering, is the name Heinrich von Lichtenstein. Closing the watch, he thinks of his mother and Jan, their lives in Vienna and graves by those of Muriel and her child—Karloff's child. He ponders the living—the daughter in

Vienna, the son in India, Earl and Caroline, happy together on the farm the nuns help tend. He likes the farm, the Sunday dinners, as he does the garden at Saint Ann's. He'll go there soon—see her bending over flowers.

Time to visit, he realizes, easing from his chair with cane in hand, finding his hat and closing the door to the clockmaker's house. The walk through town is pleasant, people waving and stopping to greet their former physician and mayor. At the gravesite, he puts a new bouquet in place of the old, no longer troubled by the past. A meadowlark's song fills the air with sweet melody. The sun is warm on his back. A gentle breeze caresses his silver hair. And there on the gravestone in the golden light, the memorial:

In Fond Memory
Theresa von Lichtenstein
Devoted Missionary
Beloved Wife
1776–1850

Final Note

Night

Tuesday, March 25, 2008: I close this account with great relief. My heart is eased, my mind at rest. And yet, I feel a press of care. Perhaps they'll mock, ignore the tale. Let all regard! The castle stands, an empty shell in the wind and rain. It knows no presence but that of owls and wolves that come when the moon is full, for those who know stay well away. And they who are young and fool enough to venture near will tell of cries and phantom visions. Gypsies call the mountain cursed. They searched the ruins the coming day; no trace or charred remains were found. The one, they say, was dragged to hell. The other? Hark! The owl will fly; the wolves depart when he appears! Should any doubt or wander there beyond the tower, down the path to the ring of bones, or think to enter in this way, they'd well behold the warning post—the sign carved out by gypsy blades! It reads (and wise all those who heed the mark): "All Who Approach Beware."